VIGIL BLACK

The Waiting Mortuary Book 2

L.V. PIRES

ISBN-13: 978-1658207409
VIGIL BLACK

Chapter One

"Go away!"

Ally Parker's voice echoes across the tennis courts as she marches toward me. Her face is tight and her racket half-raised.

I stumble back. "W-what's the problem?"

"*You*, weirdo," she says.

"What?" Only minutes before I'd been watching her graceful swing. Her moves were dance-like. Now she's unglued.

"Why would you say that?" I demand. "I'm not doing anything—just watching you play."

"You know why, Casey," she snaps. "Every day you're here watching me. I told you our lessons are over. I'm not coaching you, training you, helping you—nothing!"

"Fine, but there's nothing wrong with watching you practice, is there?"

"Yes." She turns fast and gestures back to her partner like I'm not getting it. Her blond ringlets bounce with every shake of her racket. When she turns back to face me, she lowers her voice. "I don't know what happened to you last summer, but it's turned you into a real nut-job. Even worse than before. Just look at you."

My chest tightens. I swallow and take a step back. Everyone in town knows what happened to me last summer. It's no secret that I was the one kidnapping victim in the small town of Westport who got away from the rabid serial killer, Devin Phish. It's also no secret how I managed to do that.

She snaps her gum then points one perfectly polished pink fingernail at me. "You're a mess. When's the last time you washed your clothes?"

I glance down at my hoodie and jeans. Spots of milk stain the front. I hadn't noticed until now but there's a lingering stink in the air and it's definitely coming from me.

"And your hair?"

My hands fly to my head. I try to unthread the knots.

"You need to get your life together. Take a shower."

A part of me cringes. Up until this moment, I wasn't sure anyone even noticed me. There was a time not too long ago when I had Ally's muscles. I worked out every day. My long brown hair was always in a perfect braid and when I checked myself in the mirror the image reflected back a healthy seventeen-year-old, smooth skin, pert nose, and hazel eyes, but then last summer happened.

I wring my hands as I inch closer to Ally and whisper, "There's nothing wrong with me watching you play."

"Three months of it is creepy. Everyone at school says the same thing. You've changed. You used to be okay, but now you're just freaking weird."

"I'm not—*weird*."

She laughs. "Prove it. Get a hobby that doesn't involve stalking me."

Swallowing the lump in my throat, I get ready to say something, but Ally raises her racket like she wants to hit me with it. It triggers something deeper. I grab hold of it and twist it from her hand then throw it past her. My face feels flushed as thoughts of tearing her face from her skull flash through my mind.

Her eyes widen. "You're a real psycho, you know? Just like your stupid, gay step-brother." She rushes over to pick up her racket then heads back to the court.

A sudden coldness hits my core as I move behind the large oak tree, into the shadows, and crouch, chewing on my lip and mulling over what just happened. I touch my throat and squeeze my eyes closed. *It's happened again.* I wasn't like this before the kidnapping, but something changed in me. I take a deep breath. If only I could control myself, but the thought of hurting Ally lingers. The unpredictable jolts of rage are terrifying. I dig my nails into my skin as if that will somehow release the pressure, but it does nothing.

I lean my head back against the tree and take slow, deep inhales instead. I can't let myself lose control. The wind shifts. The autumn leaves overhead sway orange and red in the cool wind. My mind flashes back to three months ago when I was taken from this very park, the summer before senior year, right after a miserable tennis practice with Ally. I touch the place on my arm where Devin Phish left bruises. If I hadn't killed him, I'd never be here right now. Somehow, I found my strength but along with that came something else more sinister.

When I peer around the tree, Ally catches my eye and shakes her head. I quickly pull back. The days in captivity changed me. Hazy thoughts of a torture chamber and morgue surface, but nothing feels clear anymore, like a photograph with faded edges or one of those old western black and white pictures that doesn't seem quite like me at all and from another time and place.

A car engine roars to life.

I dart around the tree to see Ally and her best friend lowering the roof of her BMW. Another lost opportunity. I should've confronted her. I need to let her know that she should've been the one, not me, who got kidnapped. I imagine how it would be if she had to fight for her life like I did. Not only in Phish's torture chamber in the basement of an abandoned office but then afterwards, clinging to life on a table in a makeshift mortuary.

An ache at my temple begins to pulse again—the screams pile one on top of another: *an old woman tearing at her hair, a psycho dragging a dead body, a teen holding a rifle telling me I'm already dead.* Every night the echoes of the past are there. I scream out, joining the twisted terror that lives in me, and then slam my fist into the tree. When I pull back my knuckles are bloody.

The street-lamps flicker to life. Nearly five o'clock. Things get darker this time of year. There's a part of me that wonders if I could just keep walking, straight out of town, out of life. It's not like anyone would ever notice or care. The only time I ever mattered was when I fought back and killed Phish, sawed his head in half. The thought of it sometimes horrifies me, but other times like now, when the screams start up, I remember killing him and the power it brought me, and then my head goes quiet and I can focus.

It brings a smile to my face.

Chapter Two

I *'m late.*

Sweat trickles down my back as I run through the park. The last bits of daylight fade. A twenty-minute walk to Dr. Bruner's office, but if I hustle, I can make it in less than that. The temperature has already fallen a few degrees. I pull up my hoodie and yank down my sleeves to keep my hands warm. A part of me wants to ditch my appointment. If only I could get around the whole court required therapy but considering how I dealt with Phish, I doubt there's anyone who wouldn't think I was somewhat messed up.

Heaving open the heavy, exterior door, I climb the two flights to the top of the landing.

"Right on time," Dr. Edgar Bruner says, opening his office door just as I reach for it.

Above the entrance is a camera. Bruner's always on the lookout and I have a weird feeling that it helps him stay in control. I give him a weak smile and follow him inside. The scent of his cheap cologne mingles with something more artificial that I soon recognize is the abundance of fake flowers that he has poised in vases around the waiting room.

He takes a moment to look me over.

I conceal my bloody knuckles.

Once we're in his office he directs me to my all-too-familiar seat. I ease back into the comfy chair. The tennis bracelet my mother gave me faces the wrong direction. The clasp is always supposed to hang down. I quickly fix it.

He sits across from me. "How's your week been?"

"Fine," I say.

His eyes scan down to my hand.

I tug at my sleeve.

"You need a bandage?" he asks.

"Nope."

"Antiseptic?"

"I'm okay."

"You should get it looked at."

"I will."

Court-mandated therapy was part of the deal I agreed to after the kidnapping but talking the whole time when I know I'm past the point of help seems stupid. Instead, I shift my gaze away from him and scan the room. He never does anything to change this place. There are a few nice paintings. One of a collection of children running in a park. Another of a boat on the water. Peaceful as usual, but it does little to quell the stress in my chest from missing my opportunity to confront Ally today. I was so close. On the right wall, there are three bookshelves filled to capacity with small tribal statues shoved in between texts.

"We only have an hour," he says. "We can sit here like we normally do, or you can tell me what's been going on."

I unfold my arms and take a deep breath.

He adjusts his glasses. His brown goatee is shaved precisely with matching angles on both sides. Dr. Bruner is a perfectionist. I suspect he has an organized shoe rack at home and his spice bottles all face in the same direction.

"Why don't you tell me more about your mom," he says. "Have you spoken to her recently?"

"No," I say. "She hasn't been around."

He raises a brow and jots something down on his notepad. "Stepdad?" he asks.

"Phil," I say, reminding him of his name. "No. He went with her."

Dr. Bruner purses his lips. He taps the pen against his chin before asking, "Where did they go this time?"

I don't answer right away. I'm not too keen on getting them into trouble for being away from home. A part of me wouldn't mind seeing Phil slapped on the wrist for his awful neglect, but Mom, she would be furious with me if I threw her under the bus. No doubt things would return to how they were several years ago when she withdrew her attention and left me to figure things out with my demented Grandmother.

"Casey?" Dr. Bruner snaps back my attention. "How long will they be gone?"

"Two weeks," I mutter as I check out the tropical picture on the left wall. It looks just like where my parents are right about now.

"How does that make you feel?" he asks.

I shrug and look around his office.

"Angry?" he asks.

Inevitable question. I feel my stomach churn. "It doesn't matter," I say.

"Are you sure you're not upset about them leaving without you?"

"I'm seventeen," I sigh. "I can take care of myself for two weeks." He forgets I've already seen the worst of the world. Nothing could take me down now.

He nods and again writes something then asks, "Who is taking care of you?"

"Aunt Martha," I say, a tone of irritation in my voice. "My stepdad's sister."

"And, how's that going?" he asks.

I don't know what to say. My Aunt Martha is like a noisy mosquito in my ear. "She eats all the sandwich meat," I finally say.

Dr. Bruner gives me one of his weak smiles. "Okay, but is she taking care of you?"

"I already said I don't need anyone to take care of me."

Again, he takes notes.

I shake my head. He doesn't get it. I hate being put on the spot like this. My fists clench as I take another slow, deep breath to cool myself. I can't blow this. Another jolt of rage simmers close to the surface. It has to stay hidden.

When he glances up, I'm poised again. Ready for another question.

"What about Kenny?" he asks.

"My stepbrother is fine. He's good at making dinners. I make breakfasts. Aunt Martha helps out from time to time." I don't tell him how she practically never leaves her room. "Chores get done. Prayers before bed."

There's a wrinkle in the doctor's forehead that says he's not buying it.

"We're fine," I say.

"When you were kidnapped, your parents were out of town, right?"

"Yeah, so."

"It doesn't bother you that your parents left you again, especially this soon after a pretty traumatic event?"

I rub the back of my neck.

"Do you feel anxious about anything?" he asks.

"No, why would I? Life goes on, you know?"

"I understand, but what you went through—the abduction and torture, not to mention the emotional and physical abuse doesn't just go away."

"I don't think about it."

"In here you can."

An uncontrollable snort escapes my nose as I push back into the chair. A part of me wants to talk about killing Phish, reliving the moment his skull popped in two, but I'm afraid I'll start laughing or something. Sometimes I think I won't bounce back from those images and that I'll somehow sink down into them and never return. Dr. Bruner would have no choice but to lock me up then.

I readjust my shirt. A stray piece of this morning's cereal pops to the floor.

Dr. Bruner doesn't miss it. "Okay, if you're not ready to talk about what happened, maybe we should at least talk about self-care."

"Ugh."

"You need to take a shower," he says, outright. "Change your clothes."

"I will. I've just been busy, you know?"

"These are clear signs of depression."

"I'm not depressed."

"Casey, I'm not sure you're feeling much of anything. It seems you've been stuffing your emotions down for a long time now. If you don't deal with what's happened, you're going to continue to struggle."

With both hands I slap my legs and yell, "I'm not struggling!"

His eyes widen at my sudden outburst.

I sit back while he writes something on that stupid notepad that I'd like to chuck out the window.

A tremor begins to work its way into my legs.

"Are you still taking the medication I prescribed?" he asks.

"Yes," I mutter.

"Good," he says. "That will help with the anxiety."

I take another breath, wishing I had a pill with me now. "I'm making plans for the future," I say. "I'm thinking about going back to school."

"That's a real testament to your strength," he says.

"I've always been strong," I say.

"Yes." He folds his hands in his lap. "It's one of the reasons I wanted to take your case. Actually, I fought to be on your case. Your resilience is extraordinary. Physically you've shown great strength. That's important, but I believe you're just as strong up here." He taps his head. "You'll need to remember that as we move forward into your mental and emotional recovery."

"I'm recovered, Doc. I already told you I went through something and it's over. It's gone—long gone, out of my mind. I'm focused on the future."

"You won't be fully recovered until you deal with your feelings about the past."

A part of me wants to know which part of the past—the actual kidnapping, killing Phish, or the stuff that came before that like my crappy parents.

"Look, Casey, it wastes both our time if you're not getting something out of this therapy. What is it you want to achieve while you're here?"

I nervously laugh and shake my head. His on-the-spot question rattles me. After a few seconds, I take a deep breath and try to put what I want to say into words. I feel an itch in my throat confessing what it is I need. A hard exterior isn't built overnight. Mine took years. I imagine what I'll be like in a few more and wonder if it'll be too late by then. If everything I've experienced up until now will make me so hardened to the world that I won't be able to function. I take a deep breath and say, "I want to get better."

He presses his lips together. "That's a good sign, Casey."

It's an impossible feat and one I have little hope will be accomplished. Not with the trauma of being kidnapped so fresh and the memories of what came before that difficult to retrieve. I'm more than an onion waiting to be peeled. I'm cold and hard. An iceberg. My layers congealed. Some exist, others don't. Still, I lift my head and shrug my shoulders and say, "I just don't think it's possible. You know, after what I did."

"Are you feeling guilty because of what happened to you?" he asks. "How you had to defend yourself?"

I ignore the doctor's questions and chew on the skin around my thumb.

"Because you had to do that to survive, Casey. Killing Devin Phish wasn't your fault."

"I'm a murderer, though. Right? I mean once you kill someone, you're a murderer for life. It changes you."

"You're not the same as Devin Phish. You're stronger than him."

My foot taps nervously. "If you say so."

"You saved someone's life." Dr. Bruner flips through his notes. "Patrice Thompson," he says.

Her bloodied face comes to my mind. "I remember her," I say. The college girl. The memory of her screams still wakes me up some nights. "She ditched me," I say. "Took off while I fought Phish on my own."

"She was focused on her own survival. You stayed

behind to deal with the man who nearly killed both of you. It wasn't fair of her to do that."

"It's what people do," I sigh.

"What's that?" he asks.

"Leave," I say.

Dr. Bruner reaches over to his desk. "I think we should start making a plan. You've made it clear how you want to spend your time here. I think I can help you. We'll work on rebuilding a new Casey McClair."

I raise a brow. "How would we do that?" I ask.

"You need to work on recognizing your emotions first. When you've done that, it would be good for you to revisit Kessler's Funeral Home."

My throat tightens. "W-why?"

"You'll see that it's not as scary as you remember. It's just a place where something awful happened but looking at it again in the daytime might help you work through some of those feelings you had to bury in order to survive the ordeal."

It's hard to remember anything of the waiting mortuary. Bits and pieces come to me in nightmares. A flash of a man's face. The bell tied around my wrist. The feel of the cold, hard table against my flesh.

"You'd be amazed at how quickly some of my patients have recovered from trauma by just facing their fears."

The mention of it makes me sink deeper into the chair.

"I have something for you," he says as he pulls out a black covered book and hands it to me. "You can write in here once a day. It doesn't have to be about anything particular. It's time for you to address what happened to you, the things you couldn't control. Let your feelings surface. Name them as they do."

I flip through the empty pages. There are things I'm willing to share but the chance that Dr. Bruner is going to get the full truth, including play-by-play feelings from me are slim, but a few more weeks of required therapy will turn into a few more months if I don't comply.

"Will you do that?" he asks.

"Sure," I say. "I'll write you a real page-turner."

He stands to walk me to the door. "Same time next week?"

"I'll be here." Like I have a choice.

"And, Casey," he says, before I can dart away. "Don't do too much, okay? This is a process. One step at a time. I'm going to help you build a new normal."

I quickly nod and rush down the stairs. *What an idiot.* A journal and naming my feelings. Does he think I'm struggling with a new haircut or losing a boyfriend? I begin to wonder how many other teenage girls he's helped recover from being kidnapped and surviving only after murdering their abductor?

After I leave, I head back across town thinking about how badly I wanted to wrap my hands around Ally's neck today. The way she yelled at me. The vicious words she called me. I know she wants to hurt me. She must. Why else would she have raised her racket to hit me? The gleam in her eye said it all. She's vicious just like Phish. She doesn't deserve to live. It should have been her, not me. The only thing she deserves is a cold, dark grave where she can rot.

I imagine shoving her into one, watching her tumble down and lay in broken pieces. If only I could get the courage. Then for the second time today, I begin to feel disappointed in my weakness. The torment wraps itself up inside of me. I crash down onto the street curb as cars whisk past and stomp on Dr. Bruner's stupid journal.

Feelings? Emotions? I laugh. My head falls into my hands. I rub my temples and pull back my hair. I am a murderer.

That's all there is to it. There's no changing that. I take a deep breath, then grab the journal, tear out several pages, and let them go. The pieces of paper flutter away in the wind. There's nothing to write about anyway.

My soul is long gone.

Chapter Three

"*Enough.*"

Aunt Martha snatches the milk bottle from my hand and shoves it back in the fridge. Some of it spills down my chin.

"What are you doing?" I hiss.

"You think I'm going back to the store three times this week?" she says.

The smell of her cigarette breath makes me gag. It's always a combination of stale smoke, arthritis medication, and too-strong coffee that follows her wherever she goes.

"Isn't that why you're here," I say. "To take care of us?"

"Not a bunch of pigs," she scowls. "Just look at this mess in the sink."

I turn to look at the three glasses and two plates then glance at Kenny. Calling me a pig is one thing, but my stepbrother is styling an awesome black pants and designer jacket ensemble. He's far from piggish. His dirty blond hair is slicked back like he's just come home from the salon, and there's a hint of cologne, something sporty, fresh, and familiar lingering around him.

"I'll clean the dishes," he says, stepping up to the task.

That makes me scrub a hand across my face. "Why don't you give us money," I say to her, "and we'll do the shopping."

Aunt Martha laughs. "You think I'd let you go buy a bunch of junk? You kids can't be trusted. Besides we only have enough for the basics—nothing extra."

"Can we at least get some dinner?" Kenny asks as Martha grabs the last of the sandwich meat and some bread from the fridge.

"You ungrateful kids," she mutters.

"You don't have to be here," I snap. "Kenny and I know how to take care of ourselves."

"Sure, you do," she guffaws. "Like getting yourself kidnapped?"

It's below the belt. I pull back my shoulders and step to her, but Kenny intervenes.

Aunt Martha holds up the butter knife and points it at me. "Don't do anything you'll regret," she warns. Her tight faded orange hair is like a helmet around her head. Her squinty eyes and shriveled face make me think of a late season pumpkin.

"We appreciate everything," Kenny says, easing me back into the corner.

Martha lowers her weapon. "I'd leave if I could, but someone's got to be here with you."

"Well, it's the law," Kenny says. "I mean, I'm only sixteen, so there has to be an adult—"

"Shut up." Aunt Martha shoots him a dirty look. "What do you know about the law?"

I step back to the counter.

"Look," Kenny says, intervening again, "we're grateful for all you do. Let's leave it at that."

"She's not," Martha says, pointing the knife at me again. "Been a problem for me since the beginning."

Kenny sighs. "Casey is very happy you're here to make sure we're safe."

My eyes involuntarily roll back into my head as Martha shoves the mayo in the fridge and slams the door, causing all the glass condiments to rattle. "She sure doesn't act like someone who's grateful."

"I've had my fair share of bad encounters with adults," I say, a snarky tone in my voice. "It's just nice to know that you're so different."

"Fine," she says, missing my sarcasm. She grabs her sandwich and turns to leave. "But don't think for a second that I've forgotten about your attitude." She marches away from the kitchen. A second later her bedroom door slams shut, and the sound of her favorite series revs up.

Kenny blows out a breath and goes to the sink. "You nearly blew it." He flips on the water and pours dish soap on a sponge.

I hop on the counter. "Why do you put up with her? It's not like we need her."

"I do," he says. "Just because you're almost a fully functional adult, doesn't mean I am."

I laugh. "Really? You think I'm fully functional." I point to the stains on my hoodie.

"Yeah," he says, scrubbing frantically. "You could do something about that."

"Okay?"

"Like maybe take a shower?"

"Okay!" My stomach rumbles. I open the cabinet and scan the options. "What are we going to do for dinner?" I moan. "She ate everything."

Kenny puts the last cleaned glass in the dish rack and

then helps me dig around the cabinets. After a minute or so, we find a box of macaroni and cheese.

His perfect smile lightens my dark mood as he turns to me and says, "You take a shower and I'll make dinner —deal?"

I TURN off the shower and step out.

My skin feels soft and glistens with water beads that shimmer down my arms. I wipe a hand across the mirror and clear out the steam. A part of me hates mirrors. The reflection I get never matches what I want to see. As I study my face, I feel like there might be some hope.

Even with the dark circles beneath my eyes that make me look like the walking dead, I can't help but appreciate the flushed pink tint to my cheeks and the subtle glisten in my eyes. Maybe there's a hint of muscle in my arms again, too. I know I'm getting stronger. I'm still in there —somewhere.

My mind goes back to before the kidnapping when I worked out every day and did my best to fit in. I remember getting up early for runs and begging Ally to train me for the varsity tennis team, back when I still looked up to her and thought she was my ticket to popularity. Like being popular would somehow make everything okay. I blow out a quick breath. What an idiot I was. I look down at my pale, thin legs. My calves were taut over the summer. I had the strength of a fighter. I flex my arm. A small bulge is still there but also bone and soft white flesh.

I try to shake away the thoughts of how Phish tortured me. How he forced me to fight him. How he picked me because I was strong and capable of giving him a run for his money; a real challenge—that's what he needed. Or, maybe he kidnapped me because he was searching for someone to stop him. The terror of the days of torture still feels frozen inside of me like an untouchable iceberg. Untouchable and just as hard to detect. I narrow my eyes, examining myself.

There's something emptier about me now. I'm hollow. Detached. If only I could feel something like Dr. Bruner wants but looking at myself in the mirror feels like I'm looking at someone else, nobody I know.

I pull myself back to the task of fixing my hair. It takes a couple of tries, but eventually I get the brush through the tangle and make sure to clip my nails and brush my teeth, too. No one is going to tell me that I look like crap anymore. Just as I wrap a towel around my body, there's a soft knock at the door.

"Casey?" Kenny's voice says, real gentle like he doesn't want to startle me.

"I'll be out in a minute," I say.

His feet pad away from the door.

I wait another minute until I'm sure he's gone and then slink out of the bathroom and head toward my room to put on some clean clothes.

Mom would be so proud of me. I gaze into the full-length mirror. I remember how not too long ago she begged me to get out of bed. And, now I'm up, and showering and meeting with the therapist. If only she was here to see the change. I wonder if it would make any difference if she knew. Would she quit traveling and finally stay home?

I sit on the bed and wonder what she's doing in Bora Bora right now. Probably sipping a drink or gazing at a tropical sunrise. She said she had to get away after the ordeal of the summer. It was too much for her. She said she would be a better mother if she had time to heal from the stress. I can't help but wonder who the kidnapping was hardest on. It seems everyone in the family was somehow affected.

"You dressed?" Kenny's voice asks from the hallway.

I get up and swing open the door, waving him inside.

He hands me a bowl of macaroni. "Whoa, you look … different."

"I'm clean," I say. "That's about it."

"No, you changed your clothes and your hair. You brushed it."

A smile broadens my face. I take a bite of the food, remembering how even in the depths of my despair Kenny was there to check on me. While I recovered from the kidnapping, Kenny would pull a chair to the side of my bed and read me the latest headlines from my favorite gossip show. I smile, remembering how once I even found him with a tray of tea and cookies when I just woke up from a particularly vicious nightmare.

"Did Aunt Martha complain about using the milk for this?" I ask.

He stirs his bowl of food. "She slipped out of her bedroom about twenty minutes ago, scowled, and disappeared."

"Ugh."

"She did leave us twenty bucks on the counter, though."

"Twenty?" My eyes dart to the money he pulls from his pocket. "That's enough for a pizza."

"Or, something else," he says.

I tilt my head. "What do you have in mind?" I ask.

Kenny gnaws at his lip then he takes a breath and says, "There's a party tonight if you want to go?"

My shoulders stiffen. "What kind of party?"

"High school kids—you know the ones we hate."

I pull back onto the bed with my bowl of food.

Kenny sits next to me.

His weight beside me feels strange. My bed is the nest I've built to comfort myself for the last three months. Having another person there is weird. My back stiffens.

He notices, gets up, and moves to the chair.

"I'm not sure if a party is really good for me right now," I say. "I mean I'm making progress and everything, but it might be too much."

"You've got to get on with life," he says.

"I wish I could," I say. My eyes go to what's left of Dr. Bruner's journal on my desk.

Kenny follows my gaze and asks, "Did you go again today?"

"To therapy?" I ask.

"And the other thing." Kenny's long side-eye tells me I'm not very good at keeping my daily trips to the tennis courts well hidden.

I moan and kick a pillow off the bed.

"I'll take that as a yes," he says. "Listen, Ally Parker's not going to change."

"She should've been the one," I say.

"Then Devin Phish would still be killing people. He chose someone strong for a reason. You—"

"I'm a freaking murderer."

Kenny slaps his hand to his leg. "No one blames you for killing him."

"I blame myself. I shouldn't have been put in that situation."

"You couldn't control that," he says. "You did the only thing you could."

I swallow another bite in silence for a moment before saying, "I'm just as bad as him." I stare Kenny dead in the eye. "You're just too good to see it."

"I don't know about all that." He scoops up some macaroni. "Just promise me you won't go to the tennis courts anymore."

"What else am I going to do at five o'clock every day?" I ask.

"What about night school?"

My shoulders shrug up and down on their own, a clear indication my body is just as ambivalent about moving forward as my head.

When I don't answer, Kenny slowly stands and heads to the door. "So, no party tonight?"

I shake my head no. "It's taking me a lot longer to get over stuff than I thought it would," I say, "but you know I care about you."

"I know." Kenny's face turns serious, more serious than usual. He puts the empty bowl down on my nightstand and picks up my hairbrush. "Look, Casey. We're both going to be on our own soon."

"I've got the rest of the year."

"We haven't been given much help. You know, guidance from the people who are supposed to guide us."

"I know," I say. "I'm still trying to figure everything out."

"Just keep yourself safe. I worry about you," he says.

"Don't worry about me. Nothing will ever hurt me again."

Kenny rubs his arm. His eyes are soft.

"Go get ready," I say, waving him away before he starts making me cry. "Buy something good with that twenty bucks."

He smiles and slips from the room. It doesn't escape me that he took my hairbrush and gel on his way out.

I shovel in another bite of food and lay back. Above me the swirls of the ceiling plaster remind me of my months of recovery. Too many times I stared at them and felt my life drifting in the same chaotic pattern. For a second the pang of Phish's torture flashes through my head. The way he took me from the darkened tennis courts and how frightened I was to wake up chained to a chair with the sounds of tortured victims echoing around me. A part of me can't help but wonder if Phish still has me chained up, afraid to move forward in my life.

I reach into my bedside drawer for my medication. Two pills, anxiety relief, Dr. Bruner's orders, and another spoonful of mac and cheese to forget.

Between the walls, Kenny's music begins to beat out a rhythm. I just know he's over there using up all of my hair gel.

"Kenny!" I yell and bang on the wall.

The sound of his rushing feet pound toward me.

"What?" he asks, flinging open my door. His hair stands straight at every angle.

I stifle a laugh. "I don't think you should go alone to the party. No one who uses hair gel like that should be left alone."

He waves for me to get out of bed. "Come on, girl. You need a dark eyeliner tonight. Something fierce."

Chapter Four

M*y head hurts.*

The lights in the warehouse pulse in feverish neons as some kids I know from school mingle with others, an older crowd, maybe college. I don't really know since the whole thing feels overwhelming and the minute Kenny loses me in the crowd I begin to feel as if I'm drowning in music and body parts.

My shoulders stiffen as I try to find my way to a couch, corner, or exit, but all I can do is stand and close my eyes. The sounds soak into my skin.

Phish's voice is in my ear taunting me. "*Come on*," he whispers. "*There are rules to the game—don't you want to play*?"

My stomach churns when I think of his rules. I'm in a room of broken tiles and dripping water. The floor is covered in blood. I have to fight if I want to stay alive. And then there are my sick rules, the ones I added on to his in order to survive.

Rule #1 To beat a killer, you have to be a killer.

Rule #2: Strike with a purpose.

The rules stopped there. I never made another one

after I killed him. What would be the point of another rule? Only two were needed to become who I am now—*a cold-hearted murderer*. The worst of it is I'm locked in every waking hour. There's no way out of my own thoughts. I can't forget what it feels like to take a life. Every sensation is wrapped up in that day. The feel of his warm, fresh blood sprayed across my face. The sickly-sweet scent of a dead body. The last moan of life torn from his throat.

"Hey!" a voice cries out. "That girl just freaking ran into me."

I open my eyes. There's a weird chick with red hair and high pigtails. She's staring down at me.

"Get out of the way," I say, barely keeping it together.

"*What*?" she shrieks. "You just hit me."

"No." I shake my head imagining the worst. My hands tremble as I try to center myself, but all I can think about is punching out her heart.

She waves over her friends.

Between a haze of flashing lights, smoke, and pulsing music, Ally's form takes shape. She's coming closer. My stomach clenches. I'm sure I'm going to throw up.

"Look who's here?" Ally says in a sing-song voice.

Her snide tone makes my fists clench.

"Nice makeup freak, but Halloween was over a few weeks ago."

The redhead laughs, exposing a long, white neck that I imagine tearing apart with my hands.

"Don't worry about her," Ally says to her friend over the music. "She's a psycho. Remember the girl I told you about? Harmless but super annoying."

If I could have sunk into the ground, dissolved into a puddle in that moment, I would have. I wish for nothing else but to disappear and not let my boiling rage spill over.

I lift my head. My eyes feel red. My fingers unfurl as I get ready to lunge.

"Is there a problem?" Kenny asks, pushing his way between Ally and the red head.

Ally points at me. "Your sister is the problem. Are you crazy bringing a freak like her to this party?"

"She's fine," he says. "Just leave her alone."

Ally smirks. "A whole family of freaks."

Kenny leans closer to her. "Yeah, and if you don't get out of here, we'll show you just how psycho we really are."

"You're just a kid," she snaps at him. "Whatever." Ally flips a long strand of hair and she and the redhead move past him toward the counter where a preppy kid posing as bartender cracks open a spritzer and hands it to her as if he's just done the most amazing thing of his life.

"You okay?" Kenny asks.

I frantically nod. "I need to get out of here."

He loops his arm with mine and pulls me to the corner. "Too soon?"

My head feels disconnected from my body. "I just need to leave, okay? This was a bad idea. Can I take the car?"

"Sure, I'll get a ride from one of my friends, but Casey—"

I push through the warehouse doors and out into the cold night.

Without the pulsing lights, my mind begins to focus. The music echoes behind me. There's a scent of cigarette smoke in the air. I run my hands through my gelled and stiff hair. What was I thinking? Heavy eyeliner, lipstick, freaking tight jeans and boots. There's no one in there worth impressing. I scan the lot for my car.

All around me is darkness as I climb down the docking stairs. The party was a mistake. Trying to go forward with my life was a mistake. I begin to think Dr. Bruner had it right. Maybe I can't move forward until I go back and deal with the past. If only I didn't feel so caged.

As I quickly work my way through the lot, I spot my car and a guy leaning on the hood. He's gazing into the sky. My stomach tightens, but I forge ahead anyway.

"Can you move?" I say, fumbling through my bag to find my keys.

He shifts his gaze to me. "It's too nice of a night to drive home this early, don't you think?"

I feel my face pale. Dark night. Alone. Strange guy. This is just like when Phish took me. I let go of my keys and shift my hand in my bag to the pepper spray. "Look, I don't want any problems. I-I need to move my car. Can you just—"

"You're Casey, right?" He asks with a wry grin.

I try and swallow but the dryness in my throat makes it impossible. Instead I stare hard at him and shift my weight. "Do I know you?"

"Not from school," he says, standing and moving closer.

I examine him for malintent. My grip tightens around the pepper spray as I begin to pull it from my bag. My senses sharpen, maybe too much, but I'm on high alert every waking moment and now especially. His hair is short except for the long dark bang that blocks his right eye, but even in the dim light I can see his left eye is crystal blue and there's a scar beneath running from cheek to ear. A hint of something memorable lingers in the air between us.

"Where do you know me from?" I demand.

Again, with the wry smile and then, "The waiting mortuary," he says. "You survived it."

My stomach twists. "What do you want? An autograph or something?"

"No, I just wanted to see you."

A groupie? "Leave me alone. Get out of my way."

He slides to my side. It's unsettling. His grin turns mischievous. I try to conceal my nerves. Nothing a freak likes more than getting under a victim's skin.

"How do I visit the waiting mortuary?" he asks as I push past him and open the door.

"You can't. It's not a thing. It was just a stupid room that some crazy guy set up in his house."

"Why don't they bring them back? You know, make sure the dead are really dead before shoving them in coffins?"

His tall, lean body feels like a cloak around me. The scent of sweet smoke mixes with a muskier smell that triggers something deeper. I turn to face him. "Because they know if you're dead or not. It's medical science not a guessing game."

His hand rests on the car frame. "Sure, but isn't the idea of it cool? I mean doctors shouldn't be so quick to call someone dead. Fate should decide. You might live or you might die. You linger in between, no one knows the outcome, and only time will determine which way you go. That way there's some hope left, right?"

My eyes narrow as I shove the door away from his hand. "It's sick. I was beaten within an inch of my life. Someone should have helped me, instead I was left on a cold slab with a string around my wrist."

"Sadistic," he says. "I want to know more. I'm Lance by the way."

"Good for you."

"Lance Crux. I guess we got started on a pretty dark note."

"I've had enough dark notes. I need to get home."

"Wait, don't go yet."

I set my jaw. "Back off."

"Got it." He holds up his hands and takes a step back.

I slip into the driver's seat and slam the door shut. My reflection bounces back in the rearview mirror. My mascara has smeared down my cheeks. My hands shake. I feel an ache in my chest like I'm going to scream.

Outside my window, Lance waits with his hands at his sides. His black jacket blows gently in the wind. His steely gaze focuses on me as he motions for me to roll down the window.

I shove the key in the ignition. A part of me wants to hightail it out of the parking lot. Another part of me feels stuck, bottled up, desperate for someone to talk to. Flashes of red bounce before me. My hands turn to fists as I try to push the image of Phish's bloody corpse from my mind. I look again at the stranger outside my window. I don't know if I'm meant for something sinister. If there's hope for me or not. All I know is that going home alone with my thoughts would be worse than taking a chance. I need to talk to someone right now. I slowly lower the window.

"You shouldn't drive," he says. "I mean I can see you're upset. I didn't mean to make you upset. I was just bored inside and came out here to chill. I just thought we could talk—"

"I never want to go back there," I say.

"To the party? We don't have to."

"To the mortuary," I whisper, suddenly realizing that Dr. Bruner's idea of returning to the house affected me more than I knew. "I don't even want to be here—or anywhere."

He leans closer. "It can't ever get as bad as it was."

"I don't know that."

"Why don't you stay awhile? We can talk about it."

"I can't," I say. "No offense. I just don't know you."

"Get to know me," he says.

"I don't think so."

"Why not?"

"I'm messed up."

"We all are."

"Not like me." When I turn my head, I see a pained expression in Lance's eyes. A familiar connection pulls me in.

"I have to go." I begin to roll up the window.

Lance steps back, but I can still hear him when he says, "I'll be over at the coffee shop on Main Street tomorrow morning if you change your mind. They make a really wicked espresso."

THE HOUSE IS dark when I get back. The front light is switched off. I go through the garage to get inside. There's a soft glow from beneath Martha's door and voices coming from her TV. I imagine her propped up in bed, the remnants of sandwich bread scattered around her as she half-drools in her sleep. No sense in trying to talk to her. If there's one thing I've learned about Aunt Martha, it's that she's just as absent as my parents with the extra added dose of nastiness to make my life even worse than being alone.

In my room, I tear off my too-tight jeans and fling my blouse to the floor then snuggle into a pair of sweatpants and t-shirt. In the bathroom I attempt to wash my face of the black stained mascara. I'm a horrible sight with stiff hair and darkened cheeks, but there's nothing I can do about it. After one last attempt, the mascara finally washes away to gray smudges.

I take a few seconds to stare at my bed before getting into it. Another night alone. I cringe. The voices will be waiting for me—the screams, and sometimes Grandmother at the end of my bed, standing there with her lost eyes, and I have to remember she's dead. Long dead. For years now, and I can let it go.

I quickly take two more pills and then flick off the light and slip beneath the covers. If only the medication would work faster, but it's not strong enough for my brain waves.

Lance's face appears before me in the darkness. Our conversation was weird, but he's not the first person I've met with a morbid fascination about the waiting mortuary. I think back to what he said about visiting it again. I've tried not to remember the place, even when Dr. Bruner asked me about it. There are pieces that are still foggy. I remember the bell tied to my wrist and the tinny sound it made when I shifted. I shiver just thinking about the icy metal table that I laid on, the lingering scent of death surrounding me, and then the feeling of being watched. Someone was there with me with all the control while I was helpless.

It's all I want to remember for now. Going back to the mortuary would be too much. I grab for my phone and let the soft light illuminate the darkness in the room. My heart slows to an even beat and my mind begins to relax.

The waiting mortuary was just a room inside a house on the other side of town. It doesn't hold any power. It can't hurt me anymore. Just like Lance said, nothing could ever be as bad as it was. I take a deep breath feeling the calming effect of the medication begin to take hold. I type the words, "waiting mortuary" into my phone's browser and begin to swipe through old images of waiting mortuaries from the eighteen-hundreds.

The dead lay on boards, slightly inclined, in decorative halls. It's nothing like a modern morgue. There are rows of bodies with their loved ones standing nearby. The look on the living faces is clear. They are full of hope.

I flick to another image—a woman with a bell tied to her wrist just like I had. I touch the place, tracing the circle and how it held me frozen between life and death. With my left hand, I reach over and reenact the movements of my escape. How I carefully untied the string and slipped it from my wrist, then moved from the waiting mortuary to the door past the dead corpse of a man on the second table, not knowing who waited for me on the other side. I wipe the tears from my cheeks and swipe to the next photo.

A baby placed lovingly in a basket, surrounded by flowers. His hands are crossed over his chest. There must be a mother nearby who believed he would make a return; how else could someone ignore the obvious signs that their baby was dead—his wax-white and stiff face screams of death.

My phone goes black as the battery finally dies.

Again, I'm alone in the darkness with my thoughts wondering if it's all too much for one person to bear. Carrying these memories are a burden.

As the familiar, half-grinning face of Phish appears in the darkness above me, I begin to feel a churning ache in my chest. I can't go on like this. I flip over and bury my face, wishing the medicine would numb me completely and the visions vanish forever.

"I need help!" I scream into my pillow. But who? Dr. Bruner is an idiot and Kenny is too good. There's no one but myself.

Grandmother's voice cackles beside me.

No. no. no. no. no. I sit up and reach for the medicine, downing two more pills, not sure if that will knock out the visions or me, but either way I no longer care. I just want to stop the torment. I draw my knees to my chest and rock back and forth as her image takes form in the darkness. Her bony white face leans in closer.

"Go away!" I cry. "Go away!"

Chapter Five

I *slowly open my eyes.*

The morning light pulls me from the edges of hell as I drag my feet across the bed and force myself to stand. Bile bubbles in my throat. I drink the rest of the water on the nightstand and slowly force myself from my room and downstairs for another glass.

"My head," Kenny moans from the couch in the living room.

"What happened to you?" I ask, shuffling past.

"Something pink and toxic."

"You shouldn't be drinking," I say in my most motherly tone as I slip into the kitchen and fill my glass with cold water and drink it. The coolness brings my head back into focus and washes away last night's anxieties. Beside the kitchen, there's the familiar noise of Martha's television echoing from her room.

"Any sign of her?" I ask Kenny as I head back to the living room and sit down on the couch.

He shakes his head. "She's been in her room all morning with that stupid series playing endlessly. There must be fifty seasons of it." Kenny's face is flushed red. His eyes are bloodshot and his dirty blond hair is a stiff, tangled mess that matches my own. "You think she'll ever come out of there?" he asks.

I clear my throat and say in a loud voice, "You really shouldn't be out drinking all night, Kenny. You're only sixteen. You could get into big trouble or worse you could get Aunt Martha into trouble. Imagine if the authorities found out an underaged kid was getting drunk and his caregiver did nothing about it."

The sound of Martha's door banging open echoes off the ceilings. Her feet pad closer. She stands in the hallway in her nightgown, a horrible, decades old aqua blue frock with her hands on her hips.

"Oh, sorry," I say. "Did we disturb you?"

She grimaces. "I told you two to cut it out with all your antics."

"Kenny was out at a party last night," I say. "He's hungover. Is that a problem for you?"

She grits her teeth then turns on her heel.

Kenny and I muffle our laughs.

A second later, her door slams shut.

"She doesn't give a shit," I say. "You need an aspirin?"

"Please," he moans.

In the kitchen, I fill up another glass with water, grab the bottle of pills, and return, handing him one. "How did you get back?"

"Walked." He swallows.

"Sorry," I say.

"For what?"

"I left you. That was a real jerk move."

"Don't worry. I told you it was fine." He sits up. "But what happened? One minute you seemed fine and then you took off."

"I got freaked out. I just had to get out—"

"Hold on," Kenny says with one finger in the air. He clutches his gut. "I'm going to hurl."

As he sprints across the room to the bathroom, I massage my temples and try to figure out how I'm going to make it through the day. The visions from last night still weigh on my mind and I can't keep doubling up on Dr. Bruner's pills. A part of me wants to say something to Kenny, ask for help, but I don't want to burden him with it. Besides what could he do to help me? He's just a kid. I've always been the one to protect him.

I remember years ago watching him from my bedroom window. Kenny stood outside near the bus stop. Two jocks circled him, one pulled his backpack from his shoulders. By the time I got outside, I could hear their taunts and the words they used to ridicule him. The second guy stood inches taller than Kenny and twice as big, but it didn't stop him from swiping Kenny's book from his hands and throwing it into the gutter.

My protective instincts flew into overdrive. I swung hard, clocking the taller of the two boys hard in his nose.

The injured boy's hands flew to his face and blood sprayed the front of his lacrosse jersey.

The smaller kid tried to fight back, but I kicked him in the groin, and he fell to the ground, writhing in agony.

When I turned to face Kenny, his eyes lit up.

He rushed to retrieve his book.

I never wanted to see him hurt and I'd make sure he wasn't, even from my burdens, but still they weigh heavily on me.

As I chew on my lip and pace my way to the bathroom door, the thought of going another night with the visions makes me feel nauseous. I've got to do something. I remember Lance's offer to meetup for coffee.

Behind the closed door, Kenny's retching sounds are awful.

"You okay?" I call to him.

"Yeah," he mutters.

I ease away. "I-I need to go out for a bit, okay?"

"Okay," he moans as another round of retching begins.

It's not my best plan but meeting up with Lance might be my only way to relieve some of the stress. A perfect stranger. I begin to wonder if I should try and contact Dr. Bruner instead, but shake away the thought. If I told him my dead grandmother tormented me for most of the night, I know I'll be sent away and I can't risk leaving Kenny alone or what life would be like for me in a mental hospital.

IT'S NOT a far walk to the coffee shop on Main Street.

The shop bell jingles overhead as I pull open the door. I flinch and shift my gaze to look at it.

"Casey," a voice calls out, pulling my attention to where Lance sits at a back table. He waves me over.

There's a lightness in my chest as I walk toward him and the thick, pungent aroma of freshly ground beans lifts my senses.

"I didn't think you'd come," he says as I get closer. In the daylight, his eyes reflect something even lighter, practically translucent.

"I wasn't going to," I say. "I probably shouldn't have. This is stupid. I should—"

"Sit down. Let me get you something to drink. What do you want?"

"Just a regular coffee," I say as the woman behind the counter nods.

A part of me wants to bolt. Talking to some guy I just met hours ago—*what am I doing*?

I scan the shop. There's a couch near the front window with a guy sitting there reading something on his phone. Two tables over sits an older man gazing out the window. A random cat roams between the chair legs. The girl behind the counter glances to me. Her bright green eyes flash with recognition. She refocuses and pours hot coffee into a cup. She knows me.

I dig out two bucks from my pocket and leave them for her before she can ask me some kind of uncomfortable question about my well-being or Lance can object to me buying my own coffee.

As soon as I sit, the cat jumps onto my lap, nearly spilling the hot liquid over both of us.

"Hey, there," I say to the long-haired feline.

Lance slides into his chair with two small cups of espresso. "You've got another new friend."

"Yeah, I guess."

The cat nuzzles into me, and I stroke its fur.

"Did you get home okay last night?" he asks, opening a sugar packet and pouring it into the first cup.

"Yeah. I mean I didn't drink anything at the party. I wasn't there long enough."

"But you were pretty upset."

"It wasn't a big deal."

His stare down makes me shift in my chair.

I feel like kicking myself for not saying what I need to. This is my opportunity to unload, but he's still a stranger and I have to be careful. "Okay." I take a deep breath. "I was upset."

"I hope it wasn't what I said." He sips his espresso. "I mean I think maybe I said something."

"Things are weird right now," I say. "You know what I mean?"

He smacks a hand to his head. "I'm the biggest idiot. I scared the crap out of you, didn't I? Single guy, nighttime, geez. I really need to take some sensitivity training."

"That couldn't hurt."

"Man, you should've kicked me in my balls."

"I thought about it," I say, cracking a smile. "Actually, I was going to pepper spray you."

"I guess I had it coming. Why didn't you?"

I sigh. "You said something that made sense." I lower the cat to the ground and take my coffee. The heat feels good around my fingers. "I've been dealing with a lot."

"Since the …"

"Yeah, since I got kidnapped. My therapist thinks I won't be able to move forward with my life unless I deal with what happened. And, maybe work on scrounging up some emotions about how I feel or some other therapeutic crap."

Lance presses his lips together.

A silence lingers between us.

Did I say too much? I bite the inside of my cheek, wondering if Lance knows how I actually killed Phish. Maybe he'd bolt if I told him. I want to tell him about the other stuff, too, unload all the dark thoughts that play out in my head, but no matter how cool and edgy Lance seems, I know if I tell him I have monstrous night terrors, he'd probably cut and run.

"I didn't mean to make this awkward," I finally say.

"You didn't," he says, watching me.

I can't help but stare at his scar. In the light of the day it shimmers like a silver streak, so close to his clear blue eye.

When he raises a hand to his face, I look away for a second.

"It's okay," he says, pulling my attention back. "Everyone stares. I've had it for a few years. Do you want to know what happened?"

Before I can answer, he downs the rest of his espresso and says, "Car accident—"

"Oh."

—with my folks."

"I understand if you don't want to talk about it." I cradle my coffee between my hands, threading my fingers around the paper holder.

The girl behind the counter stares at me again.

I lower my gaze as I whisper, "Everyone knows what happened to me." I tilt my head in the woman's direction.

She pretends to dry a mug.

Lance widens his eyes at her.

She turns and restacks the cup.

"You'd think they'd show some compassion or something," I say. "But it seems everyone in this town is freaked out by what happened to me—like I'm not supposed to be alive, and it somehow makes them uncomfortable knowing all the details."

"Or, it might be that you sawed a guy's head in two."

My jaw loosens. "You know about that."

"I have to say as far as defending yourself from a serious psychopath, you did this whole town a favor. They should be shaking your hand."

"You don't think I'm … a freak?"

He narrows his eyes. "Why would I think that?"

"Everyone else does."

He leans in and smiles. "You just have to stare them down. The same way they stare at you. Let them know you're just a tad bit unstable since the ordeal."

I lower my gaze wondering if that isn't actually the case.

"Am I being an insensitive jerk again?" he asks.

"No," I whisper. "I mean you're the first person I've talked to who seems to understand."

"That's because I've been through it."

I press back into my chair.

"I've seen death." He slides the second espresso cup nearer. "I understand where something like that takes you."

"W-who did you see die?" I ask, shifting again.

He pauses for a second. Beats out a rhythm on the side of his cup and then says, "My parents."

"Both of them?" I ask.

He nods. "Pretty dark stuff to see someone you love die. It still affects me. Sometimes it feels like it didn't happen to me, but someone else."

My heart sinks listening to his words. The same feeling of powerlessness passes between us. I take a deep breath. "There's something I need to ask you."

"Sure, whatever. I'm an open book."

A part of me isn't sure if I believe that he is. There's something secretive about Lance, but he's got whatever it is well hidden, buried beneath layers of smiles and relaxed gestures.

I sit up in my chair. "Did you ever go back to the accident? I mean not the accident itself, but the place where it happened."

Lance sips his second espresso. He swallows then says, "Is that what you want to do—go back to your trauma?"

His directness sends a shiver down my spine. "I-I'm not sure," I say.

"I've never been back," he says. "I was just a kid when it happened. I wanted to forget it. Move on. Do kid things and be normal, but you know what's weird about trauma? If you don't deal with it, all sorts of newer and weirder things pop up."

"Like what?" I ask.

He shrugs. "Just weird stuff."

We sit there quietly for a few seconds. My eyes narrow as I try to figure him out. He seems wounded like me—damaged in some irreversible way. When he swings his hair back from his face, my breath catches and inside I feel something stir.

"I think you should revisit the mortuary," he says. "Maybe it would help."

"I-I don't want to," I say. "I can't stand the thought of that place. What happened there wasn't an accident. It was a crime scene. Dozens of bodies were found buried in the backyard. No one got out but me."

"You wouldn't have to go alone," he says.

My eyes raise to his. "I don't know," I say, shaking off the notion. "It's a stupid idea. My therapist said it might help to deal with the past, but he's an idiot. I just want to be done with it. The nightmares and everything."

His face frowns. "Nightmares?"

I take a deep breath. It's now or never. "I guess it's weird, but I can't stop seeing the guy's face. You know, the guy who kidnapped me."

He leans back and nods. "You can't go on like that," he says. "I think you should go back and see if any of those feelings you're supposed to be having pop up. Who knows, maybe your therapist is right."

I snort and doubt it, but the mortuary seems to have a pull on me that I can't get rid of. It's more than an itch that needs scratching. It feels like something got left behind there.

Lance runs his finger inside his cup and licks the sugar.

There's something about him that makes me want to open up. Somehow even though I've just met him, his relaxed attitude even when we're talking about death, makes me calmer.

"So, are you going to do it?" he asks.

"I don't know," I say. "I'm scared, I guess."

"It's not the place that makes us afraid," he says. "It's the memory of it or maybe it's the made-up memories that really freak us out, the ones we use to fill in the gaps of what we don't remember."

"The memory of the waiting mortuary still feels real to me," I say.

The cat jumps back into my lap. As I stroke its fur, I try to imagine what it would be like to revisit the old house. To fill in the gaps of what I can't remember and then how it would be to live without fear and worry. Right now, the house feels faraway safe. As far as I'm concerned, where it's located in Bridgeport could be on the other side of the world not just a few miles east of here. I finish my coffee and wonder if I'm telling myself the truth or if this is just another way to push away my feelings about the place. A part of me wonders if it's not far away at all. If the waiting mortuary lives and breathes inside of me like some sick parasitic creature.

"You're troubled," Lance says, leaning back. "I know that look. It won't go away. The sooner you deal with it, the sooner you can move past it."

"I hate feeling stuck—the nightmares … I don't think I can go through another night of them."

"Just say the word," he says. "I've got nothing planned today."

"Today?" My pulse speeds up. Suddenly, everything feels too real.

The cat leaps away.

The bell above the door jingles again as someone new comes in.

"I-I should go," I say, pushing away from the table. "You've been … helpful."

"Don't go." Lance reaches out a hand. "We were just starting to get to know each other."

"I left my brother. He's at home and sick, and I really have to go."

Lance's gaze is soft as if he understands, and I slow down as I realize I need this stranger more than I know.

"Will you be okay?" he asks.

My chin bobs as I say, "Give me your number." I pull out my phone and quickly enter in his contact information then text him mine.

"Let me know if you need anything," he says.

"I will," I say as I shove my phone back in my pocket and turn to rush away feeling like all the people in the room are watching me now.

Why is it that the wounded are always such a spectacle? I twist my hands as I rush through the door and back home to my sanctuary as quick as I can.

Chapter Six

S*low breaths.*

It's nearly noon when I get back to the house. Kenny has made a full recovery and is getting ready to go meet his friends for lunch while I sit jittery in my bedroom trying to get up the nerve to deal with Dr. Bruner's journal assignment as a last-ditch effort to quell what feels like a surging panic attack.

I swivel my bracelet into the correct spot again. If only my mother was here. She checked on me every day after I got home from the hospital. Phil did, too, but Mother for the first time in years seemed to show concern.

It seems like yesterday when she gave it to me. I remember how she clasped the silver band around my wrist when I was ten years old and told me I'd be a great tennis pro someday. I just had to keep at it. *Never give up* were her words.

If only she didn't give up on me. Once Phil came into the picture, I drifted into second place. It wasn't long before I lost a place in her life all together.

As I flip to one of the blank pages in the journal, I take

a deep breath and begin the difficult task remembering the emotions I felt during my kidnapping.

It all began at the end of my tennis practice that day. I remember Phish following me to my car. There was something strange about the way he was acting. I wanted him to get away from me. He drugged me and shoved me in the back of his car.

Why can't I just say I was scared? I search my mind for memories of fear. All that surfaces are numbness and rage. I tear out the sheet and ball up the paper. My forehead drops to the desk. I rest it there and begin to remember how Phish made me fight him.

There were two places.

In the first place, I was forced to fight for my life. In flashes it begins to come to me. I remember the searing pain of his hits to my head. I touch the side of my chest where my lung collapsed. The ache of the wounds to my body. I search for the feelings and can't grab hold of them. All that seems to be there is a will to survive, an endurance to fight.

In the second place he took me, I was dead or nearly. The waiting mortuary comes back to me in bits and pieces. What little I can remember of Phish and the fight room is bounds ahead of what I can recall of the mortuary. The string around my wrist, the vague feeling of being watched, and then running from the house toward the ambulance. If only I could see it better and remember what I felt.

A knock at the door pulls me from my thoughts.

"Enter," I say in a muffled voice.

"Whoa." Kenny comes in. "You okay?"

I slowly raise my head. "I'm trying to reconnect to my past?"

"Why would you ever want to do that?"

"Dr. Bruner told me I have to face my past to move forward with my life."

Kenny steps closer and hands me half a sandwich. "You'll need to eat something if you're going on that journey."

I take it from him and sit up. "Why is dealing with the bad stuff so hard?"

He doesn't answer. Instead, he presses his lips together, then says, "I have to tell you something."

"What?" I groan as I take a bite of the turkey and lettuce on white.

"Ally Parker," he says.

"Stop, I can't stand her name."

"She's bashing you on social media."

"*What?*"

Kenny hands me his phone and I quickly scroll through pages of comments and messed up photos of me at my worst right after I was released from the hospital with comments like, "loser," and "weirdo" written as a caption over each one.

"What is she doing?" I demand. "I mean why would she be so cold?"

"She's a bitch," Kenny says.

"After all that I went through, she has the nerve to post pics like this—I mean she has to take them down. How do I get her to do that?"

Kenny shrugs and picks up my phone. "You could do it back to her."

"It's too easy," I say. "Besides, no one cares what I say."

"That's not true. I care what you have to say."

I ignore him. My blood begins to boil as I stand and pace the room. "Why do some people have all the luck? Why can she act like that and I'm the one who's sitting here still suffering?"

"It's not going to help if you have an aneurysm," Kenny says, forcing me to sit down. "Look, you've got to chill. Who cares about Ally anyway?"

I desperately want to say no one, only I know that's not true. Ally is like the barometer for the school. Whatever she's saying and doing is what everyone else is saying and doing. If she's happy, the school seems like a cheery place. If Ally's upset, the hallways constrict with anxious tension. And, if Ally's mad, then sometimes whole groups of students don't show up that day.

"I just wish she'd find someone else to pick on," I say.

"Maybe then you should stop going to the tennis courts every day," Kenny suggests. "You're giving her a reason."

"To bully me?"

He snorts. "I don't think anyone will ever bully *you* again."

I glare at him for a second then relax. "You're right. I'm a freaking murderer. You'd think she'd be scared to go up against someone with my rap."

"She's too dumb," Kenny says. "She's probably threatening some Middle Eastern terrorist groups, too."

"Are you comparing me to all that? I mean I've been through a lot. I'm not—"

"You're being paranoid," Kenny says. "And, she's just being a brat."

"Tell me the truth," I say, looking at him squarely. "Do you think of me as … a murderer?"

"Of course not."

"But I am one. I killed someone." I begin to twist my hands, feeling the anxiety set in. "I need to take my meds." I rush to the drawer and down two with some water then sit down on the bed and run my hands through my hair. "She should've been the one," I sigh.

"She's never going to change," Kenny says. "You need to focus on yourself right now."

There's a part of me that wants to go to the tennis courts now, confront her about the posts, but Kenny's right. I've got to focus on bigger things like my so-called recovery.

When I'm finally calm, Kenny says, "I'm going out for a while." He grabs one of my small bottles of perfume on my dresser. "Will you be okay?"

"I'll be fine," I say. "I mean I've been through worse."

"It's okay to say you're mad or sad if you feel that way."

"I'm not sad," I say. "At least I don't think I am. I don't know what I am anymore."

"You want me to stay?"

"No. Go be with your friends."

Kenny brings the perfume to his nose and inhales. "Sporty. I'm taking this."

"I can't believe you're telling me you're taking it," I say.

He waves goodbye as I flop back on my bed.

Above me, Ally's face suddenly takes shape in the plaster. I imagine taking her apart, limb from limb, and posting whatever remains on social media with the caption, "Freak."

I tear at my hair and kick the bedsheets into a little ball in the corner of my bed.

Outside my bedroom window there's something familiar. A sound that pulls my attention away for a second. I get up and look out at a few neighborhood kids running around, chasing each other and jumping in big piles of autumn leaves. I can't help but wonder what life would be like if I could move forward. If every day I didn't think about Ally and the things that happened to me.

It feels as if I'm far away from the kids below. I live on

a different planet. The sun feels soft against my face as I lean against the window frame. My room has become more of a prison than a sanctuary. I need to get unstuck. I need to get on with my life. Meet new people. Get healthy. Rejoin this world.

My gaze returns to the kids down below. They disappear into five-foot piles and bury one another. There's something there. I know that emotion. Happiness. I know I've had it before. I press my hand against the window frame. I want it again.

I quickly text Lance. "I'll meet you at the coffee shop. Twenty minutes."

Chapter Seven

I *can't believe I'm doing this.*

After I pick up Lance from the coffee shop, we begin the drive over to the other side of town. We're silent as my fingers beat out a nervous rhythm on the wheel, and I continue to second guess my decision for the entire twenty-minute drive east.

Lance glances to me and I give him a reassuring smile, but inside I feel as if I'm coming unglued. I decide to try and not think about my emotions like Dr. Bruner wants me to. At least not while I'm driving.

As soon as we cross the river into Bridgeport the scenery changes. The buildings we pass are old and uncared for. They stand in stark contrast to Westport. I take in signs of neglect—blistering paint along the sides of storefronts, sagging gutters, glass panels missing or cracked in more than a few windows, graffiti sprayed nearly everywhere, and the iron bars across lower windows which tells me all I need to know. On this side of town, the traffic is sparse. The roads are narrow and dirty.

Then, there are the people. Along the main road,

dozens of people wander the streets, some searching the trash cans while others linger near corners or outside shops. There are kids on this side of town, too, but they're not jumping in leaves. I spot a few kicking an old man sleeping in an alleyway. The elderly sit on their porches. A crowd forms outside a bustling market. A security guard or two lingers around an ATM.

My GPS tells me to turn up ahead. Once off the main drag, it feels like I'm slipping back into another era. The streets are a maze of single level family homes, all built in a similar style. The same brick patterns and formulaic rooftops remind me of how desperately everyone wanted to find comfort in similarity. Now, the structures that remain have the same familiar look of neglect.

We pass several with torn up front yards, knocked down doors, and missing roofs. A few dogs roam in and out of open lots. A garbage can rolls in the wind and against the grey, afternoon sky the trees stand stark and leafless, with brittle and overgrown branches bending toward the road.

After weaving through several blocks, my GPS says to turn left on Harwood Lane. I turn the wheel to another forgotten street.

"There," Lance says when we're halfway down the road.

My breath catches as I see it. Up ahead the sign—*Kessler's Funeral Home*—with a few letters having fallen away. It doesn't surprise me. I can hardly believe the sign still exists at all. After what happened inside, I figured they'd tear the house and sign down to avoid sickos who want just a glimpse at a true house of horrors.

I pull my car to the side. My chest begins to tighten.

The waiting mortuary looms before me. It stands there, patient, as if it has always been there and always will be.

"That's it?" Lance asks as I park the car.

"Yes," I say only vaguely remembering the structure.

"Kind of a gross neighborhood, huh?" he says as we get out.

He's right. The street is full of trash. A few plastic bags blow in the wind. Another garbage can knocks against the curb and then back into the street. The smell of rotting garbage mingles in the air along with something else more toxic. I try to figure it out. Maybe it's fuel or someone cooking drugs across the street. Who knows? A scratching sound diverts my attention. I turn just in time to see a rat as big as a small dog scurrying down the sidewalk.

I clamp a hand over my mouth.

"You okay?" Lance asks.

My head nods out a yes, but inside I feel nauseous. I shove my hands in my coat pockets, press my lips together, and try to muster the courage to move forward. I can't help but remember Dr. Bruner's warning to not push myself too hard.

"You look a little pale," Lance says.

"I'm fine. It's no big deal."

Before I know it, he pulls one of my hands from its pocket and holds it between his. The warmth feels reassuring and I can finally take a deep breath as he lets go and we walk to the edge of the property.

Surrounding the house is a large fence with a few planks knocked out along the side. I didn't have time to notice before, but now I can see how secluded the property is. How perfect it is for someone who wants to hide something. On the right side of the funeral home, there's an abandoned lot and on the left a property on the verge of collapse. Its caved in roof and shifting foundation tells me its days are numbered.

"*Marked for Demolition*," I say, reading the sign along the walk. "They're tearing down the whole block."

"Good thing," Lance says. "You never know what kind of people would want to live in a place like this."

There's something about Lance's smirk and gentle humor that lightens my mood.

"Ready?" he asks, letting go of my hand and reaching into his pocket for gloves.

I look at his long coat and boots, which are way more appropriate for a place like this than my tennis shoes, hoodie, and light coat.

We head up the cracked front walk past the tall grass and weeds. Another creature scurries in the brush. I leap back nearly falling.

Lance steadies me.

The grass shakes all the way to the road and then stops.

"It's infested," I say as we continue to the front steps and ease up the front porch stairs.

To the right is a wooden bench and milk crate. Beside the front door there's a large picture frame window. I begin to remember my escape.

"I ran out this door," I say, "and down the front walk." I take a deep breath.

Lance jiggles the front door handle. "Locked. We're going to have to be careful when we go in. A lot of these old houses have problems. Holes in the floor, electrical issues, rats."

I gnaw at my lip.

He sees my expression. "We don't have to go inside. We could just hang out here."

My gaze goes to the street. The memory of the flashing lights appears. There was an ambulance. It came to rescue me, only … I stop, remembering how Phish was in that ambulance. How it was a segue to another round of torture. I turn back to look at the front door.

"What do you want to do?" he asks.

"We have to go inside," I say. "I didn't come to this side of town and this close to the waiting mortuary to not see it again."

I go to the front window and press my hands to the glass to peer inside. Between the shades, I can make out a living room, couch, and something further back in the corner, a shadowy structure.

Lance steps off the porch and pulls up a loose brick from the front garden. "Step back," he says.

Before I can argue, he hurls the brick at the window. The sound of shattering glass echoes around us. Other than a dog barking in the distance, it doesn't seem to matter. He kicks out the shards that didn't break while I grab the milk crate and place it below the window.

"Hold on." He smooths the frame with his gloved hand, shifts the curtain to the side, and then turns to me and offers his hand.

Slowly, I inch closer. There's a lightness in my chest and my mouth feels dry. The two of us doing something secret together makes my heart beat faster.

I take his hand and step up and through the window, lowering myself to the other side into a dank and dark living room. A musty, old cigarette smell hits me hard. I raise a hand to shield my nose while Lance climbs through.

Green mildew lines the walls. A second scent seeps into my pores. Something chemical that reminds me of dissection days in science class.

"Formaldehyde," Lance says, gagging.

It brings me immediately back to last summer. My stomach churns.

Another sound in the room distracts me. There's a hole

in the corner where something feral scurries beneath the floorboards. Its scratching claws and thumping body moves around for a good minute until finally it stops at the far end of the room.

"Is it gone?" I whisper.

Lance grabs my hand and squeezes it. He leads me past what looks like an old kitchen.

Cabinets are flung open and drawers, too. A rotten smell of old food lingers, and dozens of flies zip back and forth especially near the sink. It's gross but nothing that would kill me unless I ate whatever was left in the stained white fridge.

"Gross," he says.

I shift away from the kitchen table and further into the darkened living room past scattered cigarette burns in the carpet and a torn-up couch. Its stuffing lays in clumps around the room, and I try not to think about what creatures currently occupy those spots. On the walls are what look like old army medals. An American eagle, too.

Down the hallway are two doors. We pass a faded mirror hanging on the wall.

Lance opens the first door. Old wooden stairs lead down into an even darker room.

There's something eerie about it. I feel my chest tighten as I whisper, "Close it."

He does as I say, and we go to the second door.

I push it open. There's enough light from the bedroom window for us to see.

Inside is an old bed and cabinet. It feels strangely personal. I shiver and suddenly feel like the trespasser that I am. Splatters that I know must be dried blood mark the floor and wall.

My breath catches. "This is not for us," I say, shutting the door.

"What happened in there?" Lance asks.

"I don't know the details," I say. "But It has nothing to do with me. I didn't come here to see that. Let's just look at the mortuary and leave."

"Okay," he says, his voice calm as he leads me back into the living room.

We creep further into the back of the house. We're so far back in the room now that there's hardly any light, but I can make out what looks like a coffin lying flat in the corner. My heart thumps in my chest with every step closer.

Lance tries flicking one of the switches on the wall. Nothing.

"What about over there." I point to the curtain.

We step closer and Lance reaches out a hand and pulls the old, dusty cloth covering to the side. Behind it is a glass window, but it doesn't let in any light.

As he pulls it back further, I feel myself disconnecting from my body. I can make out the shapes just beyond—two metal tables.

"You okay?" He tucks the curtain to the side.

My body stiffens.

There are two hooks, one beside each table, and a small bell with a dangling string attached to it. My hand traces my wrist as I remember being attached to one of those strings and the feeling that I couldn't … no, I shouldn't move despite the pain that ached in my chest and my eyes; they were swollen shut, and the vision of someone watching me through the window is still shadowy, but it's there. The watching chair is still there. Right in front of the window where the boy sat on guard. It's positioned facing me as if it's ready for a new occupant, someone else to watch. *I'm not supposed to be alive.* A shudder passes through me. The thought repeats in my head.

"Hey." Lance jostles my arm. "It's okay—it's over."

"I'm okay," I whisper.

"You sure?" he asks.

My head bobs, but inside I feel a single emotion fight its way to the surface.

Lance eases toward the side door as my eyes follow him.

"I was there," I whisper. "On one of those tables." My stomach twists as I fight to come back to the present. The sensation of fear feels like it's going to consume me. Every part of my body is stiff. All I want to do is run, but I feel glued to the spot surrounded by the wretched scents of lingering death and a cold creepiness that works its way deeper into me.

It's over, I tell myself. I'll never have to go through that again, but despite saying those words I still feel queasy and unsure.

Lance shoves back the door to the waiting mortuary. The bottom scrapes along the floor.

"Don't—"

Before I can stop him, he disappears inside the mortuary's interior. His dim figure behind the glass sends a wave of terror through me.

"Please come out," I whisper, but I know he can't hear me.

He runs his hands over the metal tables. "Hey, there's a bell in here," he says and pulls the string.

The ringing breaks the quietness of the room.

Inside, I feel a scream tunnel into my throat.

"I-I have to go." I turn and race back to the window and climb over the ledge back onto the front porch, crashing to the ground. Shards of glass scatter beneath my hands and knees. When I pull back there's blood.

"Casey!" Lance yells only a few steps behind me.

I scramble to the bench and tuck my head between my hands, rocking, letting the afternoon light wash over me, and the sound of a barking dog in the distance bring me back to the real world.

"What happened in there?" Lance asks as he climbs out of the house and sits beside me.

"N-nothing." I just want to get as far away from the house and this street as possible.

"You're shaking," he says. "Your hands."

"It's nothing," I say. "Small cuts."

His eyes widen as he pulls off his scarf and wraps it around the palm of my hand. "I'm sorry," he says. "I thought maybe it would be okay for you."

"No," I say. "I shouldn't have come here. It's too much."

I stand and jump down from the porch. I search for something to hit.

"Casey, wait!" he says, following me.

"This place is horrible. I want them to tear it down today. I never want to see it again."

The house's mailbox leans to its side. I rush to it and shake it from its foundation. After a few pulls, it breaks free and I hurl it to the ground and kick it hard, feeling tears rush to my eyes and the pain in my foot. A few spots of blood from my hands dot the metal.

"I'm not an expert," Lance says, his voice creeping closer, "but I think even though you're pissed and freaked out, you might be processing something."

I stop kicking the mailbox for a second and brush the tears from my face. "This doesn't feel like healing."

"I did the same thing when I lost my parents," he says. "Felt the same rage. Actually, a lot worse. I think maybe you're having what are those things? — oh, yeah, feelings."

"I have feelings," I snap. "I want to rip everyone's head

off and tear out their throats." Shaking away my tears, I realize I've just unleashed the worst of myself. Lance has seen my dark side and only on day two. Things can't possibly get worse. I turn to run away.

"Wait," he says, reaching for me. "I have an idea. Stay here." He runs to the side of the porch where a shovel juts out of the ground and grabs it. "You want to really get out your rage? Let's destroy this place."

Between tears and the sweat trickling down my cheek, I say. "How will that help?"

"It will. Trust me. You just got scared. Now, you're pissed. Come on—you'll feel better."

He's right. I'm so sick of being afraid. I'd rather unleash my fury. I grab hold of the shovel and march back up the path to the house. I climb back through the window into the darkened room. It's strange how anger protects you. Only moments ago, I fled in fear but now I'm empowered by the rage coursing through my veins.

The first thing to go is that stupid watching chair positioned right in front of the mortuary window. I stomp to it, pull back, and swing. The shovel's impact sends it flying against the far wall. There's a crack as the chair breaks apart. The guy who sat in that chair, watching me when I drifted in and of consciousness did nothing. He left me to suffer. I move closer and hit the chair again until the arm rests and legs break apart. The base of the chair collapses. I kick everything to the corner. Stepping back, I take a deep inhale and wipe my forehead, admiring my work, and then turn my focus on the mortuary itself.

"Lance?" I call out, turning to find him.

"In the kitchen," he calls back. "Sounds like you're doing a good job. Keep up the hard work."

He doesn't have to tell me twice. I raise my chin. My nostrils flare as I pull back and swing at the mortuary window. It cracks and I'm amazed one blow didn't destroy it. A long spidery web goes up and down dividing it in half. I hit it again and the fissure lengthens and spreads. One more hit and the whole thing shatters.

The rage inside of me feels alive and powerful. I laugh, hearing the edge in my throaty chuckle. My muscles quiver as heat flushes through my body.

I circle around to the entryway to the mortuary, go inside, and take a few swings at the metal tables, leaving dents in each one until suddenly the shovel comes apart. The end disconnects from the wood and drops with a *clunk* to the ground. I step back and between pants, wipe the sweat from my brow. It's not enough. I want the whole room destroyed.

The sound of clapping distracts me.

On the other side of the mortuary window Lance stands with a glass bottle tucked beneath his arm and a wicked grin spreading across his face that turns me on.

As I step from the room, I feel myself pulled to him. I drop the stick and go to his side. I feel electric.

"You've done well," he says.

"Rage," I whisper the emotion's name. "It pulses through my veins. I can feel it."

"Good," he says.

I run my finger across the width of his scar then lean closer. My lips brush against his.

"It's better than fear, right?" he asks.

His musky scent warms my senses. He's the best smelling thing in this room. I feel his returned energy course through my body.

He pulls the bottle from beneath his arm. "Let's get drunk."

But I feel as if I'm already drunk. His touch on my arm

and warm, soft lips against my own mingles with the adrenaline.

"Come on," he says as he leads me through the living room and into the kitchen.

"Where did you find this?" I ask.

"In the cabinet," he says, "while you were busy taking out your rage." He unscrews the cap.

"What is it?"

He takes a deep inhale. "Whiskey."

Something about this moment feels surreal. It's different from the agony of darkness that I've lived with for the last three months.

Lifting it to his lips, Lance takes a long drink. His cheeks flush red. He hands me the bottle.

"I'm not much on whiskey," I say, not having tried it before, but I don't want this moment to vanish. The power I feel needs to go on.

A thin coating of dust covers the glass bottle as I take it from Lance's hand and breathe in the woody smell.

"It burns," Lance says. "But in a good way."

I take a huge gulp. He's right. It burns like fire down my throat and into my stomach. My eyes tear as I choke out, "strong", then pass it to him and wipe my mouth.

Lance drinks again. He doesn't gag.

My hands find his again and the moment we touch I know he can feel the connection between us. Our chaotic and crazy worlds feel distant when we're together. Even in this shithole with rats, mold, and death, I feel safe with him and more importantly, I feel alive.

He leans closer.

I part my lips.

His warm kiss has the sting of whiskey.

I take the bottle and drink again. This time it doesn't burn as bad. The pathway from my head to stomach is torched with alcohol. Again, my fingers find Lance's and trace the white, shimmering trail of his scar. I lean closer and kiss his cheek. His eyes reflect back the same need I have. Between drinks, I let my pain dissolve as his kisses take away the ache of thinking about the past.

SHE'S NOT AN EASY CATCH, but finally I see her lying there strapped down to the waiting mortuary table. She struggles against the straps as she slowly begins to wake.

"Ally," I laugh, hearing the sinister cackle in my own voice.

Her eyes widen.

The stick of the shovel is all I need and with one good swing I pull back and bring down the hard edge with full force onto her arm. The bone cracks.

Her screams soon follow.

I haven't forgotten the way she raised her racket to me.

Her cries feed my anger.

"I'll give you my car," she begs.

My stare turns cold.

"What do you want? Popularity?" she cries. "Fine, I'll give you friends."

I raise my chin and bare my teeth.

Her eyes widen. "Stop!"

"You would do this if you could," I hiss as she moans and tries to get out of her restraints. It's no use.

I raise to swing again and hear the crack as her other arm breaks.

A curdling scream echoes in the waiting mortuary and feeds me. I pull back a fist to my mouth, covering the insane, shrill staccato of laughter that erupts from deep inside of me.

"Stop! Stop! Stop!" Ally moans.

My eyes narrow and the pulse in my veins flows steady and confident.

"Let me go, Casey," she cries. "Please!"

Her screams trigger something in my core and the buried pain that grew through my own torture. I feel frothing at the corners of my mouth. All I want to see is her blood and pain.

Again, I raise the stick and bring it down hard on her skull.

A gasp and then a gurgle slips from Ally's throat. Her eyes roll back and her face pales.

I toss the stick to the corner and step closer to examine my work.

Blood trickles from her scalp down her cheek and pools onto the mortuary table. I reach up and grab hold of the bell's string and tie it to her limp wrist then slip out of the room and find my chair.

It's time to watch and wait.

Chapter Eight

The *wind ruffles my hair.*

A faint sun dances through heavy, grey clouds. A long string of drool dangles from the corner of my mouth. Beads of water form on my bare arms. A dull ache pulses at the base of my skull and as I slowly sit up, I feel the dryness in my mouth and a sudden surge of blood around my skull.

"Where am I?" I moan. I take in the garden around me.

A lawn covered in brown leaves. Patio furniture, a pool filled with murky green water, and a tarp half covering it. Beside me, a white statue of cupid looks down at me with curled lips.

The taste in my mouth is death. My shoes are caked in mud and my hoodie is torn at the sleeve. Several small cuts line my palms and fingers.

I search for my phone, but it's gone and then in flashes I begin to piece together my last memories. A whisky bottle and Lance's lips on mine. The waiting mortuary. As if I'm watching a movie, I begin to remember something far worse: *Ally's blood-curdling cries.*

My stomach twists. I lean against the cupid and throw up. Alcohol and vomit mingle sending me stumbling backward to the wet ground. I press my fingers to my temples as I try to get my bearings.

It takes every ounce of will to move forward and not fall to the curb as I emerge from behind someone's house. The sun pushes through, leaving shadowy prints on the pavement.

Up ahead, a man emerges from his front door. He's dressed in a maroon robe.

I know him. I'm on my street. He lives a few houses away.

I slide behind a parked car and wait for him to go back inside.

It's morning, but how?

The last thing I can remember is the afternoon with Lance and the waiting mortuary. I've somehow lost track of time, not just a few hours. A whole night is gone. I look at my hands. The veins stand out blue against my grayish white skin. I feel the same veins in my neck. My thoughts turn to Lance. *Where is he? I have to find him.* My heart flutters as the fluids in my body slosh to find equilibrium. No, I have to take care of myself first. I have to get home.

I peer around again. The neighbor stretches and turns to go inside. Once the door is closed, I get to my feet and walk as fast as I can to my house.

With every step I feel the lining of my stomach bubble and the sour taste of bile creep back into my throat. As I near the house, I spot my car parked at a strange angle in the driveway. My hand shakes to my head as I try to remember if I drove or not.

Hurrying to the back door, I search for the spare key. My fingers fumble in the dirt, digging for the shiny metal until finally I find it and quickly wipe off the dirt and shove it into the lock, but then as if by natural force the door swings open.

Martha stands there like a sentinel guarding the threshold. Her brow furrows. “Where have you been?”

I push past her. “Not now.”

She waves her hand in front of her face. “My god, you’re drunk!”

Her words fall on deaf ears. Whether I’m still drunk or not is the least of my worries. I need my bed, my nest, my sanctuary. I stumble up the stairs.

Kenny emerges from his room, yawning. “Casey?”

“Not now,” I mutter.

In my room, I quickly shut the door, the world, and my thoughts. I down two of my pills, strip off my dirty clothes, a scattering of mud and leaf debris falls to the ground as I kick off my shoes, and disentangle several leaves from my hair.

Once done, I climb beneath the covers. I need everything to stop for a second. I need to remember what happened, but not now, not with the sting of a raging headache forming an attack on my brain. I push back my anxiety, forcing myself to believe everything will be fine, but no matter how hard I try the flashes of Ally’s screams begin to penetrate between the forgotten hours of my life.

What happened in the night? I have to find out, but the memories are gone. They’re all gone, as vanquished as my understanding of what’s real and fantasy. Flashing in front of me is red and Ally’s twisted and agonizing expression as she begs for her life.

My hands shake as I search my bedside table for my phone. I must have left it here, somewhere. I need to talk to Lance. I have to find out what happened last night.

It's not next to my bed. Not there. I try to remember the last time I saw it, but the dull ache in my head throbs and seems to block out any logical thought.

There's a gentle tap at the door.

"What is it?"

"Just me," Kenny says.

"Hold on."

I throw on some sweatpants and a long-sleeved hoodie, anything that doesn't reek of whiskey and vomit. "I'm a little sick," I say as I crack open the door.

"I need to talk to you," he says. His eyes are strained.

"No, not now. I just need to rest."

He rubs his brow. "Where were you last night?"

"With a friend."

"All night?"

"I really need to be alone right now."

"Martha's downstairs pacing," he says. "She might leave."

"Good," I whisper. "We don't need her."

Kenny chews on his lip. "I think there's something you need to see."

"Can't it wait?"

"No."

I take a step back.

He pushes into the room.

"Listen, I got a little drunk last night. I'm not feeling the greatest."

Kenny holds up his phone for me to see.

My eyes are a bit blurry, but there's no ignoring the words.

TEEN GIRL GOES MISSING.
FEAR OF ANOTHER KIDNAPPING
SENDS PANIC THROUGHOUT WESTPORT.

I back to my bed and feel like I'm drowning in a sick nightmare. Heat rises from behind my eyelids. A weight emerges from the air and presses down on my shoulders and beads of sweat form at my brow.

"I-I didn't do it," I say, waving for him to put the phone away.

His eyes are full of questions. "I didn't say you did."

My stomach twists. I look down at my red palms. There's an embedded splinter from the wooden end of the shovel beneath my skin. My hands rub together. I twist them as worry takes hold. There's only one way out of this. I have to find Lance. I have to find out what happened. "Have you seen my phone?" I ask, pushing back the sheets on my bed. "I have to call someone. I have to find out—"

"Are you okay?"

"No," I shake my head. I rub the heels of my hands into my eye sockets then let my arms fall fast to my sides. "Just tell me what it says," I demand. "I need to know." The gaps in my night are like a hundred little nooses.

He raises the phone and reads on. "Local tennis star, Ally Parker, disappeared last night around five o'clock from the same location where a previous kidnapping took place. Her car door was found open and the keys in the ignition. When she didn't return home in the evening, her parents reported her missing to the local authorities. Anyone with information should contact—"

"Enough," I say, running a jerky hand through my hair.

A sudden banging at the door sends a jolt to my heart. "What are you doing in there?" Aunt Martha yells.

"Leave us alone!" I yell back. "Why is she always around when I don't need her? Oh, god!" I moan and flop down in the corner chair. Half of me thinks I just got too drunk last night. The other half wonders what I did in my blackout. Revisiting the waiting mortuary was supposed to bring peace. Instead its stirred a hornet's nest of problems.

Kenny rubs his chin. He stands in front of me waiting for me to open up to him, but I can't. He'd never understand. Telling him what I'm thinking would only make him afraid of me.

"Do you want me to call your doctor?" he finally asks.

"No." I go to the mirror. My face is ghostly white. I turn back to face him. "I've been to the tennis courts everyday but not last night. I swear!"

He shifts his weight and eases himself onto my bed. Onto my sanctuary. My eyes widen.

"Where were you then?" he asks.

I want to explain it to him, but it's impossible. No one but Lance could ever understand what it feels like to see death, to be hopeless and scared. "You've got to understand," I say. "I didn't do anything to Ally. I promise. Help me. Everyone will think I did it. Her friends will tell the police. They might come asking questions. You've got to say I was here all night."

He glances down at his phone. "It says she was taken yesterday evening."

"I was nowhere near the courts yesterday evening." I gnaw at my finger. I'm sure I was still at the funeral home with Lance.

He knits his brows. "Then why won't you tell me where you were?"

There's a pressure inside of me to say something. I push it down. "I-I can't tell you. Just please if anyone asks, say I was here yesterday afternoon and night."

"Sure," he whispers, but I know that look. He's upset. Withholding information separates us. I'm losing his faith and he's all I've got.

As he begins to get up, I reach for his hand and pull

him back onto my bed. I stare into his eyes. "You don't know how scary it would be for me if I was taken to jail. It would be just like it was when Phish held me prisoner." I hold one of my wrists imagining the handcuff he put on me. "I just don't think I could handle it."

Kenny's gaze turns thoughtful. He reaches out a hand and lightly strokes my arm. "I just want you to be okay."

My chin quivers.

"I'm sure you'll be fine," he says in a reassuring tone.

I press my lips together and lower my gaze to keep him from seeing the torment brewing inside of me. He doesn't have a clue what's been going through my head for the last few weeks and I vow to keep it that way.

He squeezes my hand. "If you need someone to talk to—"

"I know," I say. "You've always helped me. I know you were there when I came home from the hospital, in the late nights while I healed. I never said thank you, but I remember you were at my bedside. You stayed all night holding a washcloth to my head. Helping me through the nightmares. I appreciate everything you've done."

"I was worried you wouldn't make it."

"You don't have to worry about me anymore," I say. "I'll be okay."

"When are you going to come out of there?" Aunt Martha screams out again.

I pull back my shoulders, get out of the bed, and march to the door. When I open it, she stands there with her arms folded across her chest.

"What?" I demand.

"You're not going anywhere until you tell me where you were all night."

"I was here," I say.

"You think I'm stupid."

"She was here," Kenny says, coming to my side.

Her glare narrows and I try to keep my composure. "I just went out for some coffee, but I didn't have enough money to get any."

She raises a brow. "And, the smell of alcohol all over you?"

I reach to my nightstand and grab a towel. "I don't know about that. I was just on my way to the shower. But I'm glad you're noticing me for once." I push past her.

Martha hisses, "You good for nothing brat."

As if on automatic, my hands turn to fists.

Kenny grabs me by my hoodie. "I think you just need a nice, warm bath." He pushes me gently in the bathroom and waves goodbye as he closes the door. His voice is mocking as he says to Martha, "kids."

A few moments later their feet pad away in separate directions, and I flick on the shower, desperate to wash away any remnants of the night before. If only it was that easy to just wash everything away. I let the warm water soak into my hair and aching muscles and lather the soap across my skin lifting the dust and dirt of the mortuary. The water at my feet turns brown. A few minutes later I step out and towel off.

I wipe a hand across the steamy mirror and look hard at myself. *Who am I anyway?* Only a year ago I was a tennis player, good student, strong, independent, and full of hope. Now, my face bounces back a different image. The answer is clear: *lost.* I shake away that idea. As I run the brush through my hair, I force myself to remember last night the way it should be. I reclaimed my power. I destroyed the mortuary. And, there was more. My fingers rise to my lips as I remember Lance's kiss. No one has kindled that feeling in me before. I want to live in that feeling of last night.

I have to find Lance.

Chapter Nine

"*Where are you?*"

The minute I find my phone in the back pocket of last night's jeans, I tap out the message and hit send.

"Come on, Lance," I say, pacing. "Please answer."

Martha lingers somewhere around the kitchen corner, listening in.

I move away from her prying ears.

Twenty minutes pass as I gnaw away at my finger. Then, finally when I can't stand it a second longer, I grab my bag and the keys then head to the car.

"Where are you going?" Martha yells, hot on my heels.

"Out," I yell back then slide into the driver's seat and lock the door.

I pull out the driveway while Aunt Martha stands in the front yard, arms crossed with a familiar scowl splashed across her angry face.

There's no time to deal with her. Right now, I've got to get across town and find Lance. It's nearly noon. My thoughts wander to him still lying on the cold wooden floor of the funeral home.

The lunchtime traffic snarls around the interstate.

My phone lights up with a message.

"Where are you going now?" Kenny texts.

I ignore his question for now. No answer is better than a lie.

The car ahead of me is slow to turn. When finally it goes, I manage to get onto the interstate that will lead to the bridge and the other side of town. Swerving across two lanes of traffic, I make it to the fast lane and punch my foot down on the gas.

As hard as I try to talk myself down from the ledge of worry, flashes of Ally's tortured expression still pop up on every billboard advertisement I pass.

"*Why would you do this to me?*" she cries out.

My eyes widen. Day terrors—that's all this is. I push away the image of Ally lying somewhere between life and death on the waiting mortuary table. "I didn't do anything to you," I mutter. "You got yourself in trouble. I didn't do anything to you."

In the next billboard, a model reclining on a couch with a bottle of designer water sits up. Ally's face replaces hers. "*You really messed up*," she says. "*You could've had it all. I would've given you friends*."

"I don't want your friends," I say.

Her image reclines again with a bloody wound to her head leaking grayish brain matter in big, fat drops to the ground.

My hands stiffen. I flick on the radio to distract myself.

"It's nearly Thanksgiving," says the announcer. "What are you thankful for?"

Static disrupts the commercial and then suddenly it's Ally's voice saying, "Not you— *murderer*," she hisses.

My fingers fly to the buttons as I frantically work to change the station but the word, "*murderer*," repeats itself on every channel until finally I flick it off and feel my cheeks flush red and my grip around the wheel tighten.

I drive faster, speeding around slower cars until up ahead I see the exit for Bridgeport. I try to swallow, but my throat is still dry and the acidic taste of last night's binder clings to my tongue.

A few more blocks and I'll be there. I turn the wheel and head down one of the side streets. My heart speeds up. I veer around a rolled-up carpet in the middle of the street while next to me a man wearing a military jacket approaches my car window. One of his sleeves is pinned halfway up. With his one hand he reaches out and taps on the glass next to my head.

"You want me to wash your window?" he asks, showing a scattering a yellow, broken teeth.

"No," I say as I try not to roll over his foot.

"Got a dollar?" he asks. "I need to get some food."

I gnaw at my lip. Just as I reach toward my bag, my phone lights up. I grab for it and flick to the message.

Another one from Kenny. "They're here," is all it says.

Cops. I just know it.

The phone falls from my hand. I wave away the guy next to me and twist the wheel to get around him. Once I'm clear, I follow the back alleys toward the mortuary. I'll find Lance. They'll find Ally. Everything will be okay.

When I get to the old house, I quickly park and jump out, racing back up the front walk.

"Lance!" I call out as I climb through the broken window. The familiar scent of stale cigarette smoke is there along with something new and charred.

When there's no response I rush to the kitchen. The empty bottle of whiskey sits on the table. I spin back to the living room. A rustling sound from somewhere in the house makes me pause. I press my elbows into my ribcage. My fingers flutter at my side.

"Are you here? Lance," I whisper.

Even though it's dark, there's still enough light to see the shadowy outlines of furniture. I step closer toward the waiting mortuary. My hands fall away as I slowly work my way past a trail of destruction. Some of it is there in my mind. I remember taking out my rage on the house. I don't remember destroying most of the living room, though.

Where there had been a side table and couch, there's now nothing but torn fabric and wood and along the side of the wall, a large burn mark goes from ground to ceiling. I stare at it a moment as if somehow that will bring back some idea of what happened here. It's not beyond me to have wanted to burn the whole house down.

I reach for my phone and text Lance again. "I'm here, at the waiting mortuary. I'm looking for you. Where are you?" I hit send hoping to hear a *ding* on his phone somewhere in the house. Instead, it's quiet. As eerily quiet as it had been yesterday before I stirred up more mess for myself.

Easing away from the charred wall, I begin to walk to where the mortuary curtain is now drawn closed. The chair I demolished is there. Dented and broken, it lies like a fallen soldier in the corner. Two of its legs remain intact. The other two lie scattered at opposite ends of the back room. My hands sweat as I reach for the chair and remember the rage that filled me only the night before. It looks like a simple chair now, nothing more.

I leave it on its side and turn toward the window. If only I could leave all my rage here. Let it be torn down just like this house.

My fingers trace the edge of the curtain. Its dusty, dark

fabric is coated with a thin veil of green mold that smells like Kenny's wet socks. If not for the dampness in this house, I'm sure the fire from last night would've torched it to the ground. I slowly pull back the curtain and gaze through the hole that had been a glass window only yesterday.

The table is empty.

I breathe a sigh of relief and laugh. No Ally. No tortured body or splatters of blood. My fears got the best of me, but now I know they're just that—fears. I spin around and slap a hand to my forehead. The torture I put myself through and for what?

Suddenly it dawns on me that Ally probably faked her disappearance for attention. Of course, that's it. It's near the holidays. She probably wants a new car or a ski vacation. It's not beyond something she would do. Meanwhile, I'm sitting here driving myself crazy in this old, disgusting house.

I go to the mortuary's side door. It's half torn from its hinges. I force it back and go inside the room. The walls pulse in shadowy outlines that would normally send shivers down my spine, but now as I stand there, I begin to feel the sensation of control. Standing in the room that made most of my worst fears manifest, and now I can see it for what it really is. Just a room. An old house. A room—nothing more.

Dr. Bruner was right. Lance was right. I take a deep breath and blow it out. I dealt with the past. I shake my head. It's just a room in a house. It holds no power. For the first time in months, I begin to feel lighter. The worst of the night is that I got drunk.

I clasp my hands to my chest. I'm healing. I'm getting stronger. I laugh and take the bell down from the hook and ring it. The sound still bothers me, but it doesn't own me anymore. I leave it on the dented metal table just as the sound of breaking glass comes from outside the mortuary window.

"Lance?" I say as I rush out through the living room and into the kitchen.

The empty whiskey bottle lays in pieces, smashed on the ground. I turn back to the front window. An animal or the wind must have knocked it over.

I sigh and ease my way to the waiting mortuary one last time. Coming here again wasn't for nothing. At least I've faced it on my own. I take a second to imagine putting all my worries away and what life will finally be like then glance to my phone.

Nothing. Lance must have found his own way home. A part of me wonders if he'll ever text me back or if that's it. Maybe he just wanted to see the house and get a quick hook-up.

As I turn to leave, something in the corner catches my eye. I notice the chair near the waiting mortuary. The broken, unrepairable watching chair that I destroyed the night before. It lay on its side only moments before, but now … I step closer. My eyes widen. Two of the chair's legs are gone yet it stands upright perfectly balanced.

My hand trails to my throat. I stumble backward and fall to the floor. My bracelet breaks from my wrist and scatters beneath what remains of the couch. I cry out and fall to my knees, searching madly for it. With every reach I only feel the wooden floor and years of dust and rat droppings. As I rock back on my heels, a gush of tears pours down my cheeks, then there's something else that pulls my attention back to the waiting mortuary window.

As I slowly stand and wipe my cheeks, my eyes latch onto something standing beyond the window. A darkened figure with yellow eyes hovers there. Its gaze burrows into my core. I feel the hair on the nape of my neck bristle.

"L-leave me alone," I stutter, slowly backing away.

Then the watching chair shifts on its two legs. It slides several feet and stops when it's positioned squarely in front of the mortuary window.

I stare blankly.

The wood of the chair creaks. The two good legs shake as if there's weight pressed into the seat. The bell rings.

My mind scatters as I turn to run. An icy flutter sweeps at my hair. I feel something grab the nape of my neck, but I don't stop. I run, breathless to the window and fall out onto the porch, pull myself up, and rush into the street as the sound of a screeching car echoes in front of me.

Chapter Ten

I*'m frozen.*

The tires screech. The bumper stops within an inch of hitting me. The car door opens, and a grizzly looking man steps out. "Why don't you watch where you're going?" he shouts.

My head twists from the mortuary to his car and then to mine. Rattled, I dart to my car door, unlock it, and jump in. My breath is heavy as I try to calm down, but I can't get the image of those yellow eyes out of my head.

As the stranger drives away, his middle finger extended to me in clear view, I yell out, "Screw you!" and let my head fall back against the rest until suddenly there's a tapping at my passenger window.

I jolt upright.

"We have to talk," Lance says. "Open the door."

"What are you doing here?" I hit the power locks, and he gets in.

"Drive," he says.

"I-I can't," I cry. My head falls to the steering wheel. Will I ever have peace? I glance to my wrist. My bracelet is gone. Tears begin to form, and I feel my tight grip on the wheel loosen as I raise my head.

"What happened?" he asks, scanning my face.

My voice won't work. I try to form words but every time I open my mouth nothing comes out.

Lance takes my hands. "You're ice cold." He begins to warm them between his own, even blowing his hot breath on my fingers. It makes me relax a little.

I rest my head back then shift my gaze to the old house across the street. "The house," I manage to say.

"Yeah, it's messed up," Lance says. "We trashed it pretty good."

"There's something wrong with the house," I say, turning my face to his.

"It's never the place," he reminds me. "It's just what we tell ourselves about it."

My throat feels dry as I pull my hands away and wipe the wetness from my cheeks. If only he could've seen what I did, but I refuse to let the last few minutes in the house ruin my sense of control. "Why are you here?" I say as I try and pull myself together.

"You texted me."

Right. I shift in my seat. "Last night," I begin, "is a blur."

Lance's sheepish smile reemerges as he whispers, "Not to me." He takes my hand again and begins to massage it. "I only had two sips from the bottle."

"I-I don't remember much after you gave me the whiskey." I try to not sound accusatory, but there's a tone in my voice I know he doesn't miss.

He leans against the window. "You think I messed you up?" He shakes his head. "No, no way!—you drank almost the whole bottle. We only made out for a little bit before you started talking about some girl who really pissed you off. Told me to take you home, so I did."

I feel stiff again. "What did I say?" I whisper.

"Just that it should've been her, not you."

"I say a lot of things. It doesn't mean anything."

Lance raises a brow. "Okay."

I tap on the wheel then ask, "How did I get back to Westport?"

"I drove your car. You told me where to go. You jumped out before I could walk you to the door and disappeared behind your house—"

"*My house*?" I say, embarrassed and desperately searching my mind on why I didn't just go inside. Why would I wander into the neighbor's yard? "It wasn't the afternoon by then, was it?"

"Early evening, I guess," he says. "Man, that girl Ally really bugs you, doesn't she?"

"Why do you say that?" I ask.

"You told me all the horrible things she'd done to you. You said she deserved to be dead. You even told me some of the ways you wanted to hurt her."

My eyes widen

"Do you still feel that way?"

"No," I snap. "I was drunk, just talking. I didn't mean—"

"Then I saw on my phone this morning that some girl named Ally got kidnapped last night, and I couldn't help but think it may have been her."

I rub my hand on my leg. There are answers I need from last night, but the way he's looking at me right now is like how everyone in town does, like I did something awful. "Listen, I don't remember you driving me home. I don't remember getting out of the car. I don't remember—

"All right," Lance says, in a calm voice. "But you're okay now, right?"

I find myself taking deep breaths and turning my attention back to the house. I'm not sure.

"You got wasted, Casey," Lance says. He reaches to me and weaves his hand through my hair cradling the base of my neck and drawing me closer to him. "You got out some of your rage last night, that's all. It's part of dealing with the past, letting old wounds heal. You can let it go now."

His words are tonic to my worry even if I'm not sure I can believe anything he says or worse yet, anything I tell myself. But, letting go is all I've ever wanted.

We stare at one another for a moment. Our connection, at first strong, now feels unbreakable.

"Are you done with this place?" he asks.

I take a deep breath and glance back at the house. The yellow tape that surrounds the property flutters in the wind. Soon, it will be gone, and the mortuary will be leveled to the ground. The past will be nothing but a faded memory then.

"I think so," I say as drops of rain begin to trickle onto the windshield.

"Want to follow me to my house?" he asks.

Just then I remember Kenny's last text. The cops have to be asking him a million questions. "I should get back home," I say as I quickly reply to him saying I'll be home in twenty.

Kenny responds a second later, "Don't come back."

"Why?" I tap out and hit send.

There's a long wait between texts and then, "Aunt Martha told the cops you weren't here last night."

Of course, she did. Traitor. If only Ally would show up, then this whole thing would be over.

"Problem?" Lance asks.

"You know what—I need to hideout for a few hours. Going home right now could make things … complicated."

NOT LONG AFTER, I'm following Lance's directions to where he lives. I drive down a small side-road, wondering if I know what I'm doing. There's no doubt there's something between us, something strong that feels like it could be magical. I begin to wonder if I'm ever going to be able to balance my instincts, what's real and what's not.

Surrounding the dirt road are hundreds of bare trees standing against a rainy, foggy mix. The day's dampness feels like it's soaking into my skin. I turn up the heat.

Finally, a sign looms up ahead. *Welcome to Willow Oaks*. I pass a dozen or more signs that line the drive offering incentives to move into the complex. *Two months free rent. Pets Welcome. No Security Deposit.* At the very end of the road a group of apartments stand huddled in one unit, no more than twenty set against a tree-lined backdrop. A few lights glow along the side of the building. One flickers like it wasn't installed correctly. A bulldozer and a few other machines sit off to the side. A dozen more units stand half-built nearby.

I park on the gravel.

"It's one of my favorite places," Lance says. "Quiet here—peaceful, especially when the construction crew takes the day off."

The rain has stopped but fog begins to rise from the nearby river and clings to the woods. Other than the crunching of our feet on the gravel, the complex is silent.

"It's all new," he says. "The apartments. Brand new.

They're still building. Supposed to be a pool going in behind my apartment next week."

I turn to follow where he's pointing.

"You live here, by yourself?"

"Yeah," he says, waving me to follow him.

My feet hesitate. A part of me wants to leave. It would be safer to leave. But if the police want to question me, and Ally's playing it up for attention, maybe the safest place to be is somewhere like this. Remote and hidden.

I follow him into the apartment complex's darkened corridor. The sound of our shoes against the hard cement ground echoes against the walls. The smell of freshly cut wood and paint mingles and is a welcome relief to the old musty smell of the mortuary.

"It's the last door," Lance says.

Once he opens the door, we walk inside to a short hallway that leads to the living room. A plush couch, glass table, and oak cabinet are the first few things that catch my eye. I scan the rest of the room taking in the artwork on the walls and stylish lamps on the side tables.

"This is nice," I say, sliding a finger along the granite counter. "How do you afford this?"

"I work," he says, flicking on a light.

"But, you're only seventeen."

He shrugs. "I work hard." He comes to my side and reaches for my hand then guides me to the couch.

The smell of new fabric mingles with Lance's musky scent. I pull away and look back to the kitchen from this new angle. Stainless steel appliances and the quiet thrum of a super modern ceiling fan make me begin to wonder.

"Do you really live here?" I ask, raising a brow.

"For now," he says.

I gently push him away not sure what that means and

go to the window. The blinds are slightly parted. Outside I stare at the deep hole in the ground where the pool will go.

"Where did you live after your parents died?" I ask.

"With my grandmother," he says.

"So why don't you live with her now?"

He's quiet at first and then says, "She died a few years ago."

"Sorry," I say. "It's just that—"

"You don't trust me."

"I don't know you."

"I'm not complicated," he says. "What else do you want to know?"

I take a deep breath. "Where did you go after your grandmother died?"

"A foster family," he says. "Until last year when I got a job and moved out."

"And, that's it?"

"That's it."

But I know it's not as easy as all that. Losing his parents and then his grandmother must have been hard. Still, he managed, and I admire the strength in him. It's something I recognize in myself. Something that you only get when you've had to face something tough before you were ready. Not everyone survives, but the strong, like us, do. And we recognize each other. It's like a scar on the underbelly; you never show it off but it's still there, still noticeable by others with a similar wound.

"I'm sorry about your grandmother," I say.

"She taught me a lot," he says. "I only wish she hadn't died. There was more I wanted to know about her, but I never got the chance."

My eyes flick back to the pool outside. Some people get lucky. One person has horrible parents and the next gets a decent family, someone to love them, tuck them in at night, make sure they're okay. The only person I ever had to care about me was Kenny and now here I am, letting him handle the police when it should be me stepping up to the plate, telling them that Ally Parker is a big, fat liar and I had nothing to do with her disappearance.

"What are you thinking about?" he asks.

"Families," I say. "How they're all so different. My parents are always gone. They like to travel. They'd rather been somewhere half-way around the world than with me."

"That must hurt," he says.

"I've got my stepbrother," I say. "Kenny. He's the only person who's been there for me. Then there's my Aunt Martha. She's watching us while my parents are away."

"How's she?" he asks.

"Horrible," I sigh. "She makes my life a nightmare. For some reason she's always hated me. She blames me for everything, but I guess I haven't been easy on her either." I remember how I ditched her that morning and wonder if I shouldn't make an effort to try and smooth things over with her. I glance at the time on my phone. "I should probably go."

"Really? So soon? You just got here."

"It's not a great time for me."

"You've said that." He smiles. "It's never a perfect time ever to meet someone new, but …" He pauses as his crystal blue eyes shift away from mine like he's searching for how to express his feelings.

I take it all in. Lance doesn't run from his fears. Not like me. He's braver to say it. Not like me. I'm trained to push it down and away, cover it up, and hide.

When he looks back at me, I can see the depth of what stirs inside of him. In one moment, he's a puzzle and in the next something like a soul mate.

"I really like you," he says, drawing me closer. "I don't want to lose you."

I let him wrap his arms around me and he feels like a blanket to my fragile spirit. He feels protective and safe, but I can't shake what worries me the most: *Am I drawn to something dangerous yet again?*

My hands slide up his chest. I feel the beat of his heart beneath his coat and slowly help him take it off then run my hands up his neck as he tilts his head down and presses his lips against mine, and for a few minutes as we stand there in front of the window with the soft rain starting up again, I feel safe.

They say you meet people where you are in life, and I can't help but wonder if we are meant to heal one another.

Chapter Eleven

"S*he's still missing.*"

Kenny's message flashes on my phone as I'm already heading toward my car. It's the third message he's sent since I told Lance I had to leave and promised him I would text him before bed that all was okay.

"What's going on?" I text back.

"They just left," he says to my question about the cops and "Aunt Martha is going insane."

For Kenny to say Aunt Martha's going insane means something. He can usually calm her by turning the conversation to an episode of her favorite television show or brewing her a nice, hot cup of tea.

"She locked herself in her room," Kenny says as I flick through the messages at the stop light. I'm tempted to text back, "good" but instead I bite my tongue.

"I'm on my way back," I text and hit send.

I can't help but wonder where Ally is hiding while the attention around town stirs. Probably with some guy she met. I try to stifle the urge to post something snarky on her social media page.

At the next light, I flick through her recent posts. All fake smiles and air kisses. Her best friends post pictures of themselves with candles, saying there will be a vigil for her to raise attention about her disappearance. Already the post has three hundred likes. It stings when I think about how no one did anything like that for me.

Finally, blocks away from home I slow down and cruise closer to make sure all the cop cars are gone, then pull into the garage.

Inside, the house is quiet. Martha's door is closed. Her show blares at top volume. I wouldn't be surprised if she called my parents and they listened politely then hung up and went back to their beachside cocktails.

I slink up the stairs and quietly go to Kenny's room, knocking gently on his door. When he doesn't answer, I slowly turn the knob.

"Can I come in?" I say as he sits up in bed.

His silence must mean he's pissed. I gnaw on the inside of my cheek as I try to think how I'm going to make it up to him.

I scan his room. Perfect as usual. Not a stray sock or sweatshirt on the ground. A chemistry book is propped up on his desk next to three sharpened pencils and a calculator. If only I could be as organized as him. The familiar sporty scent of my perfume lingers in the air. He closes the book he's reading.

"So, where were you?" he asks.

"I had to take care of something," I sigh, slowly lowering my bag to the ground. "Sorry about that." I'm on the verge of telling him about last night. About meeting Lance, going back to the mortuary, and losing whole blocks of time but before I can, he says, "You don't have to tell me."

I twist the cuff of my shirt and sit at his desk. "Any news on Ally?"

"Nothing."

"The cops were here?" I ask.

"Two detectives," he says.

I shift in his chair. "What did they ask?"

"They wanted to know where you went and what we knew about you following Ally to the tennis courts every day."

"It must have been awful," I say. "I shouldn't have—"

"It wasn't bad," he says, propping up his pillow. "The best part was Martha about crapped her pants. She thought you got kidnapped again."

A slow smile broadens my face. "I'm sure that would've devastated her."

"When she heard it was someone else who got kidnapped, she pretty much ignored them until they said you were one of the suspects in Ally's disappearance."

My stomach twists. I shake my head. "I know how it must look," I say. "But I think I know what's going on?"

"What?" he asks.

"I think Ally's faking it."

Kenny tilts his head. "What do you mean?"

"How much do you want to bet Ally's off at some spa right now and doing this to set me up?"

Kenny laughs. "That would be the ultimate revenge bitch move."

"I wouldn't put it past her."

"You know, now that you mention it," he taps a finger to his lip, "you did annoy her a lot especially in the last few weeks. I could see her setting you up."

"And, getting all the attention when she gets back."

"Diabolical." Kenny grins.

I nervously scratch my arm. "What else did the detectives want to know?"

"Basics. I told them you were here all night."

"Thank you."

"Then Aunt Martha said you weren't." He looks away. "I guess I could've done more to keep her quiet."

"It's not your fault," I whisper. "Do you still believe me?"

"If you said you didn't kidnap her, then why would I think you did?"

"I'm sure her friends have it out for me."

"You're probably right. I wouldn't go on social media any time soon."

"Too late. I saw they're having a vigil for her."

Kenny perks up. "Let's go. We can dress in black."

A part of me stirs at the idea of going in all black to Ally's kidnapping vigil, carrying a single candle in hopes of her safe return only to have her reappear the next day, and then I could rejoin the group in her welcome back and say, no I'm not at all offended that you thought I was capable of doing something that horrific.

As if Kenny senses my excitement, he gets out of bed and digs through one of his drawers pulling out a black veil and handing it to me.

I step to the mirror, draping it over my head. "Please, return my dear friend, Ally Parker," I say in a melodramatic tone as if speaking to the camera.

Kenny raises the back of his hand to his forehead. "We can't go on without Ally's constant torment. How will the little people know their place?"

As I slide the covering over his head, Kenny continues his monologue and there's a pang in my chest as I reach for his hand. It's cold. When he finishes, I say, "I shouldn't have left you to deal with the police."

He pulls the veil from his head. Blond tufts of his hair

stand ruffled.

I smooth them back. "It was a real chicken shit move," I say. "I knew they'd consider me a suspect."

"We're not guilty of anything," he says, "but they keep trying to make us think we are."

"I know," I say. "The weak always get destroyed first."

"We're not weak," Kenny says, jerking my hand.

My eyes search his as I pull back. "I just meant—"

"I know what you meant," he says. "You're the kidnapped victim and I'm the gay kid brother. We're different than the others. That's what you meant by weak?"

I turn away from him for a second, gathering my thoughts. I'd never thought of myself as weak before the kidnapping, but his reaction caught me off guard. Maybe I misunderstood Kenny. Maybe he's angrier than I thought. When I turn back, I lower my hands and say, "You're right. I'm being stupid. You know what? We're the two strongest damn people in Westport—screw them!"

Kenny slides back in his bed. He reluctantly smiles as I ease my way beside him and say, "I'll talk to the police tomorrow, okay?"

"They want you to go down there."

I nod okay and nervously look away. I have to get Lance to go with me. That's the only way they'll believe I didn't have anything to do with Ally's disappearance. If only I could remember the whole night, start to finish, it would make things so much easier.

As I stand to leave, Kenny says, "You don't think it's another serial killer, do you? I mean like a copycat or something?"

My shoulders stiffen, but then I relax. "No way," I say, a reassuring tone in my voice. "Get some rest, okay?"

He slowly nods as I grab my bag and head down the hallway to my room. I flick on my bedroom light and look around, feeling on edge. Two pills and a quick change of clothes, then I slip into bed and try to relax.

For a few moments I lie there and wait for the faces to form in the dark. I listen for Grandmother's cackle and Phish's bloody head to appear. When they don't come, I begin to wonder if revisiting the waiting mortuary has somehow vanquished them forever.

I feel my wrist. If only I had the courage to go back inside the house one more time for my bracelet. A part of me begins to wonder if Mother will be upset about it and the thought of her coming home to see it gone makes my chest ache. Still, I could never go back in, not with those wicked yellow eyes I'm sure I saw in the waiting mortuary and the strange way the chair shifted into place. Even sending Lance in would've been cruel.

Just as sleep begins to weigh heavily on me, I remember I forgot to text Lance that everything is okay like I promised him I would.

I reach across to my bag and dig around for my phone, finding it at the bottom.

As I begin to type, a black smear smudges the screen. I try to rub it off, but it only gets worse. I sit up and flick on the light. Something must have spilled in my bag. As I rifle through my purse searching for an uncapped pen or spilled bottle of mascara, my fingers brush against something sharp. I yank my hand back and look down at my skin. Smears of red coat my fingers.

My throat tightens as I slowly take my bag and flip it upside down. The contents spill onto my bedsheets.

Makeup, pens, wallet, change, and then … there … I feel a sickening churn in my stomach as I slide back. It can't be.

Beside my phone is a perfectly manicured finger. Shellac pink just like Ally's.

Chapter Twelve

"*They found her in pieces.*"

My eyes flit from Martha to Kenny.

The morning newscaster's voice is serious as he goes on. "The local girl, Ally Parker, who went missing less than two days ago has been found dead. Investigators discovered several remains of Miss Parker inside a hollowed tree in a local park where she was known to play tennis on a regular basis. Officials are concerned that another predator may be on the prowl and warn citizens to be vigilant after dark."

In the background stand several girls, Ally's friends. One begins to howl.

"Oh, look at that," Martha says. "Is that who the detectives were talking about? Pretty girl, *Tsk, tsk.*"

Kenny raises a brow. His stare-down makes me chew nervously on my thumb. Then I start to think about the finger, Ally's finger wrapped in a sock and stuffed inside my jewelry box and stop chewing.

"Well, there you go," Aunt Martha declares. "That's why you don't go out after dark in a town like this. A bunch of crazies running around. Now, who's going to accuse you of doing *that*?" She snorts looking at me. "As if you could cut up a body."

I slowly stand and pace behind the couch as the newscaster shifts from the girls to Ally's parents. Their grief-stricken faces are lined from what looks like a long two nights without rest. My foot taps nervously against the couch.

"Can you stop that!" Aunt Martha yells. "You're shaking the whole room."

The ceiling gives me as much hope that everything will be okay. I tilt back my head and feel the hot tears slip out and slide down my cheeks. I quickly wipe them away.

Martha doesn't notice, but Kenny's looking at me.

All I can think about is the finger. The grayish tinge to the dead flesh was horrifying against the perfect nail. I remember flipping it over with a pencil, examining it, until I was sure it was Ally's. The long night of worry sent me spiraling. All the previous day's progress came undone in the night as Phish's voice reemerged and taunted me to fight while Grandmother sat in front of me cackling. Then, from what felt like nowhere, Ally emerged—her head dangling strangely from her neck, two bloody stumps of fists pounded against my bed-frame as she cursed and insulted me.

As the night progressed into early morning, I rocked myself in my corner chair trying desperately to find some quiet, a bit of peace to work out what I was seeing in front of me. The thought of downing the rest of my pills went through my head more than a dozen times. The voices encouraged me to do it. I don't know what stopped me other than the thought of Kenny finding my dead body in the morning. I couldn't do that to him.

Instead, I focused on remembering the night in the

waiting mortuary. When would I have had time to kidnap and kill her? Plus, I'm not strong enough like Martha said, but Phish's voice was there by my side to remind me of how I'd found the strength to fight and kill him. "If you could do that to a man of my size, surely you could take that wisp of a girl."

I shook his words away. "I couldn't have killed Ally," I cried.

"You murderer!" screeched Ally. Her broken arms jutted out in opposite directions.

Phish weaseled closer, whispering that he had watched me that night. He had seen what I did. It excited him. He wanted more.

Flashes of the waiting mortuary pressed harder into my skull and refused to let go. Each one of Ally's screams brought forth something new. I remembered the crack of her bone as I brought the shovel down on each of her arms. Then, I heard the moan she made as her life slipped away. She lay on the waiting mortuary table for hours as I watched. She dangled between life and death. Over and over again, the memories of the night I killed Ally merged in and out of dream state and reality.

"But the finger," I muttered. "How did I end up with her finger in my bag?"

Grandmother cackled as she was next to take the position beside me. Her long grayish white hair did nothing to cover her naked body and her hollowed out eyes shone with the blackness of hell. She whispered to me a story of when I was a child. Late in the night when it was dark and lonely like now, I had prayed for Grandmother's death, for her to finally be gone and the agony of her nightly screams to end. In a swift and violent motion, Grandmother yanked a clump of hair from her head and pressed it into my hand. "A memento," she cackled, and then I remembered.

"I snapped her finger, didn't I?"

Grandmother's eyes bulged as she threw back her head, exposing the blue and green veins of her splotchy skin and laughed again.

Yes, I said to myself, defeated. I took Ally's finger—a memento, a keepsake, a souvenir, something to remember another kill. *It was me—I must have done it.*

Desperate, I sat down at my desk and wrote a letter in Dr. Bruner's journal. Lance Crux brought me peace of mind. He was the only good thing to happen in years and now everything's falling apart again.

"A real shame," Aunt Martha says, breaking into my thoughts and bringing me back to the present. "She looked like a nice girl. Why couldn't you be more like her?"

"You mean dead?" Kenny asks.

I wrap my arms around my waist. The living room feels hollow and cold, and I can't help but wonder how much longer it will be before the detectives appear again on the doorstep. I grab my phone from the side table and quickly text Lance, "I need to see you."

Martha slaps her leg, stands, and turns to face me. "You better not have done anything to her," she warns as she walks past us and into the kitchen.

"She didn't," Kenny says. "Maybe you could support her once in a while."

Aunt Martha guffaws from the kitchen as Kenny shuts off the television and makes his way to my side.

"You don't look okay," he says.

My lips tremble. I don't want to say it, but I need help. "I think I killed her," I whisper.

"No, no, no, you didn't," he says. "Don't ever say that again."

"What's wrong with me?" I ask him.

His eyes go to the television then back to me. He quickly grabs the remote and flicks off the news. "I'm not an expert or anything, but I think the kidnapping is triggering you, okay? I'm going to call Dr. Bruner."

It feels like a lifeline. It's as if I'm drifting farther and farther away. Kenny sees me. He'll help. I feel my fingers reaching out and grasping for his help.

"Okay," I whisper, but before he can leave, I reach out a hand to him. "What am I going to tell the police?"

"Just tell them you were here the whole night like I told them."

"But she won't say that."

Kenny narrows his eyes as Aunt Martha comes back in the room.

She shakes a bottle of water at me and says, "Those detectives yesterday said you might have something to do with this."

My head feels warm. Her accusing beady eyes burrow deep into me.

She folds her arms. "So, you're going to go down to that police station and tell them where you were the other night."

It feels as if I'm coming unglued. Maybe Aunt Martha's right. It pains me to feel that. My eyes flash to Kenny. He'd do anything to help me, but whatever happened to Ally has to be somehow my fault. As I slowly stand and head to the stairs, I come to the realization that if I admit to stalking her and even the torturous vision, I will somehow be set free from my own torment.

"Casey," Kenny follows me. "You don't have to say anything."

"You don't need to protect me," I say to him. My eyes

search his. "I just need you to stay out of this." I begin to go up when Martha comes closer.

"Are you going to talk to the detectives?" she asks.

I swallow and take a deep breath. "The truth is …" I say to Aunt Martha, nervously fidgeting with my phone.

Kenny jumps up two stairs to my side. "That she was out with a friend that night."

I'm on the verge of taking Kenny's hand, leading him the rest of the way upstairs to the jewelry box, and showing him Ally's finger, but instead I say, "That's true. I was out with a friend, but I'll talk to them, okay?"

It seems to satisfy Martha. At least for the moment. She nods and goes back to her room while Kenny raises a brow.

"You sure?" he asks. "If you wait, I'll go with you when I get back from school."

My heart feels like it might implode, but I mask my worry and nod out a "yes" then hurry upstairs.

In my room, I stare at the jewelry box. If I don't go to the police, they'll come for me. If I do go to the police, I'll be locked up for sure. But what other choice do I have? It won't be long before the detectives return, maybe even with a warrant. I can't spend another night here projecting the images of the dead.

I envision myself—the murderer that I've become. Once a murderer, always a murderer. I sit on my bed then quickly stand. My sanctuary feels toxic. This room is sick. I'm sick. I can see that now, but as I imagine explaining my version of things to the cops, I know where it will lead me, and I refuse to be taken again, captured, handcuffed, and tormented, thrown into a five-by-five prison cell to rot.

I take the jewelry box from the shelf and shove it into my bag then grab a change of clothes and a few other things. A picture of Mom. A get-well card Kenny gave to me in the hospital. The only tennis trophy I ever won in ninth grade, and then I open the journal Dr. Bruner gave me and write out a note, "*I'm not going to jail.*"

Chapter Thirteen

"I *need to see you.*"

It's not a clear plan, but I can't stay at the house. Going down to the police station isn't going to happen, either, and disappearing out of town forever feels daunting. If only Lance were here to help guide me. As I step from the coffee shop, a huge cup of extra strong java in one hand, I feverishly text him with the other that he should meet me as soon as possible.

"I have to go to work," he texts back a few seconds later.

"It's an emergency," I say. I chew on my lip and slip into my car. When he doesn't text after that, I begin to rub the back of my neck. An empty feeling forms in the pit of my stomach. The last thing I want to do is scare him away. In between long sips of coffee, my hand taps out a nervous rhythm on the steering wheel until I see a police cruiser pull into the spot behind me.

My whole body stiffens. Two large men get out. Once they go inside, I start the ignition and slowly pull away from the curb.

A new plan forms. If I'm fast, maybe I can catch Lance before he leaves for work. I retrace the drive from the night before, remembering the turnoff to the new apartment complex only a few miles north of town.

As I pull my car around the winding road, I begin to feel the familiar foggy thinking and stress that comes after staying up all night and down another few sips of coffee then search my bag for my bottle of pills only to remember that I forgot them in the dresser drawer in my bedroom.

I slam a hand on my thigh. I blow out a quick frustrated breath, knowing I'll have to return to my house to get the rest. It's not the end of the world. I try to remember that I can handle things. No reason to freak out. As I scrounge around the bottom of my bag, I find a few scattered pills there. I take two and wash them down with a gulp of coffee. It will only last a short while, but it might be long enough to get me away from the chaos brewing around me.

In the daylight, Lance's apartment complex stands more clearly against the tree-line. The construction crew is back at work. A bulldozer up ahead clears ground while several men in hardhats carry supplies from a truck to an open area where the framing for a new structure already stands.

I park my car in the gravel lot and get out.

The air has the crisp, clean scent that reminds me winter is not far off. The sky is blue and full of white wispy clouds. The wind feels brisk as it rustles through the trees. I quickly reach back inside my car and grab my coat.

There are only three other cars in the makeshift lot. Far from full occupancy. A woman's voice pulls my attention to the opposite end of a long, paved sidewalk. She stands in a brown pants suit with a couple who are holding hands. The woman waves them to follow her and they disappear into one of the corridors of the new building as I slowly close my car door and make my way to Lance's apartment.

Walking the familiar corridor feels like moving through a wind tunnel. The air is strong. It ruffles my hair and makes a whistling sound as it goes through the eaves. I pull the collar of my coat close around my chin.

At his door, I rap gently and wait, digging my fingers deeper into my pockets. There's no answer, so I knock again and step back. There's not much time to figure this out. Soon the detectives will return to my house. They'll find I'm not there and then what? My license plate will be tagged. Every cop in the state will be looking for me.

"Lance," I call out, pressing my ear to the door. I quickly text him again, "I need to talk to you" then step around the side and peer into his window. Again, I tap gently on the frame, knowing that if he finds me doing this it will freak him out, but I'm desperate. When there's still no response I feel my stomach tighten. There's nothing left to do but wait. If only he left me a key I could hideaway inside until everything blows over.

I try the door again and search beneath the mat for a spare key. When I don't find one, I run a jagged hand through my hair. I have no other choice now. I can either wait for him to come home or face up to what I've done on my own. I wring my hands. I need him. Without his alibi, the detectives will never believe me.

Just as I'm about to head back to my car, a fluttering pink ribbon zips past me. Carried by the breeze, it sails into the air then back to the ground, dancing across the pavement until it stops and gets tangled in the grass.

My eyes narrow. The wind shifts again and lifts the ribbon inches above the ground. I ease myself away from the wall and follow it. It flutters delicately. I reach out and try to catch it, but the ribbon sails away and descends into what will soon be the swimming pool but is now a large, empty hole in the ground. I go to the edge and stare down. It's at least ten feet deep right now. The foundation hasn't been laid. It's nothing but dirt and water. The ribbon sinks into the muddy bottom.

As I begin to turn back, a strong gust of wind pushes me hard to the edge. I fight to regain my balance.

"*You killed me*," Ally's voice drifts in the wind.

My spine stiffens as I flail my arms.

"*Murderer*," she hisses.

Her shrill laugh penetrates my skull. Dirt from around the edges begins to crumble as I cry out, "Help!" then twist and tumble halfway over, feeling the air knocked from my lungs. I dangle there, clinging to the cold, wet ground until I can breathe again and then with one hand I reach up and pull myself to level ground.

"*It should've been you*," she says. "*You did this*!"

Panting, I quickly cover my ears, but her voice is still there. Not just in the wind but in my head. I cry out, "Just leave me alone!" and push myself up, half covered in mud, then rush back to Lance's apartment door.

"Excuse me," the woman in the brown pants suit calls out from the end of the hallway.

I back up and clutch my coat. Beads of sweat form at my brow. "I-I'm just looking for my friend," I say.

"Who's that?" she demands, walking closer.

My legs tremble. I steady myself against the wall. "He lives here. His name is Lance."

"That's impossible," she says. "I haven't rented anything out yet in this complex. They're still building it. Besides, we're only taking applications for the furnished apartments."

My muscles tighten as I suddenly feel foolish. I stammer, "I-I'm sorry. I thought he lived here."

Her eyes narrow and she looks me up and down. "Wait a second," she says, only feet away now. "I know you. I've seen you here before."

"N-no," I say, stammering. "I have to get back to my car."

She pulls a phone from her pocket. "You know what? I've had enough of trespassers. You stay right there. I'm calling the police."

It feels as if the world is caving in on me. I push past her and run to my car.

Chapter Fourteen

C*old coffee.*

With a jittery hand, I raise the drink to my lips.

It dribbles down my chin. I wipe the back of my sleeve across my face and neck. My muscles twitch as I return the cup to the holder.

For ten minutes I've watched my own house. No sign of the police. If I rush in and grab the medicine, I can be gone, on the road, and out of town in just a few minutes but something holds me back.

Reaching into my bag, I take out the jewelry box, shove it into the glove compartment, and then text Kenny, "I need to know you'll be okay."

It takes a few minutes but then he responds. "What does that mean?"

I slowly draw in a breath. "I'm leaving."

A few seconds pass then, "I'll go with you. Don't go without me!"

My shoulders drop as a wave of regret washes over me. I'm not like my parents. I slowly turn off the ignition. If there's anything I've learned from the past few months, it's that I can't ignore my feelings. I think of the power I felt when I went back to the mortuary and reclaimed my anger over fear. Right now, I'm afraid. Deeply afraid and nervous, but on top of that is my concern for Kenny. Leaving him without an explanation would make me just as bad as my parents—no worse. They never even feigned concern. Kenny is my whole world, and I won't leave him.

As I head inside, Aunt Martha lingers in the living room. "The police were here again looking for you," she says. "I thought you were going to talk to them."

"I was going to," I say. "I mean I will talk to them soon."

"I told them you were on your way downtown. Now you've got me lying to the detectives. Figures."

She's right. I haven't been fair. I've let everyone shoulder the trouble when it's me who should be stepping up. "I need to talk to Kenny first," I say, heading toward the stairs.

"He's not here. Have you forgot? It's Monday. He's gone to school."

My hand grips the railing. I can't wait for him to get home. It'll be too late by then. A note. I'll write him a note.

"Where did you go just now?" she asks.

I swallow and ignore her.

"It wasn't to see *Lance*, was it?"

There's an awkwardness between us as I try to figure out what she's playing at and how she knows his name. Before I can answer, she clucks her tongue.

"Thought you may have," she says. "Heard you say his name yesterday."

My eyes follow her as she slowly stands. "I know that boy," she says. "He's no good for you. You've got to get rid of him."

My shoulders stiffen. "You don't know him."

"Lance Crux, right?" she asks.

I slowly nod.

"He was in a car accident with his family a few years ago, right?"

My jaw unhinges. I'm not about to open up to Aunt Martha, but I can see she's fishing for me to say something. When I don't, she turns and walks back to the couch and sits.

Reluctantly, I take her bait and follow her. I grab a pillow and hold it in front of me as I lower down to the couch.

"How do you know about Lance?" I demand.

She stares hard at me and then says, "From a few years ago. Then, it was in that little journal you keep upstairs. The same one that said you weren't going to jail."

"That journal is private."

"You've been a secretive little minx for days now," she says. "You think I'm not going to poke around to find out what you've been up to?"

"You have no right." My shoulders tense. I hate her deep in my core.

She narrows her eyes. "All this coming and going and you know what I think?"

I press my lips together. Not the least bit interested in what she thinks.

"Alright, I'll say it. I think you're involved in something. Over your head with that little friend of yours, Lance Crux. Did he tell you about his parents?"

There's a nastiness in her voice. Her sharp tone repulses me. "He did," I say.

She leans closer. "Did he tell you he killed them?"

I swallow hard and avert my gaze. It's lowdown, a new level of perversion, even for her.

"That's what they say," she goes on. "He made that

accident happen. Took the wheel from his father's hands and plowed the car into the embankment. It flipped twice and he should've been killed, too, but he wasn't. Hardly a scratch, they said. He watched his poor parents die. It was even said that his mother had a chance. She begged for help, but he climbed out of the overturned car and let her scream herself to death. He's a real sicko, you know?"

A dull pain begins in the back of my skull. There's no way anything she's saying is true. I remember the softness of his touch. The way he reassured me.

"The authorities took him over to Bridgeport Hospital after that. He was one of the youngest kids in the psych ward, stayed there for months from what I was told. They let him out when they said he was recovered, but to tell you the truth I don't think that ever happened."

My hands begin to tremble at the mention of Bridgeport Hospital.

"I hope you get rid of him," she says. "It would be for your own good."

"Why do you care?" I ask, defensively. "It's none of your business."

She slides to the edge of the couch. "It's definitely my business," she says. "And, you're going to put an end to it right away."

"But, why?" I ask. "I'm nearly an adult. I can choose who I hang out with."

Her eyes widen. "It's never a dull moment with you, is it?"

I slowly stand. "I know I'm not a perfect, but you can't tell me who I can talk to."

Martha leans back. Her hands go wide on the back of the couch. "Who knows what that boy is capable of," she says. "If you ask me, based on what I know, I think he's capable of anything."

"You don't know him," I snap.

"Oh, is that so?" Martha's tone goes up an octave.

As I turn to leave, she jumps from the couch and grabs my wrist. "You just think you know everything, don't you? I think I've had about enough of this, you little brat!"

My core turns black as she continues her verbal assault. "You should be careful," I hiss and yank my arm away.

"What's that supposed to mean?"

A storm churns inside of me.

"I think I know what's going on." She hovers over my shoulder as I turn to get away from her before I do something I'll regret. "You've done something, haven't you?"

"You don't understand—"

She snorts. "I know enough," she says. Her lips pucker. "That's it. I'm calling the police and then I'm leaving. You are on your own."

I clutch my arm. I'm so close to getting out of here. I have to keep her from calling.

"I've had it," she says.

"You don't understand." I rush to her side before she can pick up her phone. "I'm going to talk to the police. Don't call them, please!"

Martha ignores me.

I spin back to the stairs and dart to my room. There's no time to waste. I climb the stairs, two at a time, rush into my room, yank open the bedside table, and grab my pills.

Just as I turn to leave, there's a click. I slowly go to my bedroom door and turn the knob, only it won't open. I twist harder. The overwhelming fear of being locked in a torture room sinks back into me.

Phish's voice comes from behind and when I slowly turn, he's there. A sinister grin on his face. "Let's play," he begs.

I turn back to the door and yank on it, screaming, "Let

me out! Aunt Martha, let me out!" I begin to pace the room, wearing out the similar path I walked last night, avoiding Phish's taunts.

There's a loud bang downstairs and yelling. Martha's throwing a fit.

With my phone still in hand, I jab out a text to Lance, "Please, help me! My Aunt Martha has me trapped in my room. I can't stay here!" When he doesn't respond, I know that's it. I'm going to jail. The metal around my wrists feels real. The provoking taunts of my jailer will only force me to do the inevitable. I can't wait for that day to come.

I pour a handful of the pills into my palm. The note is still on my desk. "I'm not going to jail," I say aloud and take the pills in my mouth.

THERE'S nothing more deafening than silence.

No screaming in my head or thuds of bodies hitting the ground. Not even a car's engine passing by outside or the sound of Aunt Martha's series playing in the background. When it's quiet like this, I feel hollow. My body vibrates as I lie stiff on my back like I'm in the ground, buried alive, without the chirps of crickets clinging to the trees in the cemetery above or the sobs of visiting relatives coming to say their last goodbyes.

I try to move my fingers—there's nothing. My mouth is dry. Not even tears form as I lie in the darkness and wait for this nightmare to end. All I have now is my mind. Thoughts pass through me of lying like this for eternity. No one will come for me. No one will care. It's all up to me to survive and fight back—that's what life is, isn't it? Just one big fight from start to finish.

If only I could make my voice work. I try to call out to Kenny. Nothing works. I need just one sound. A gust of wind would be enough. A creak of the house would break this spell. The sound of the heat kicking on would shift the painful monotony. I wait and stare blankly at the ceiling as the minutes turn into hours. All I can do is think and wonder if I'm still alive or if this is what it feels like to be dead—an eternity of staring, watching, and waiting for someone to remember you.

Then the ringing of a bell.

The sound wakens me from my prison and I slowly stand from the grave and take the small device in my hands, silencing it, but the reverberations are still all around me filling my head with horrible images of Aunt Martha tied to a metal slab in the waiting mortuary.

She is there on the table, twisting back and forth as I tie her down.

My hands tighten around her neck. I squeeze her throat tight. My sinister laugh masks her gasps.

Martha tries desperately to twist away. Her tied hands flutter back and forth, but my grip is strong. Her eyes bulge and red blood vessels begin to line the whites of her eyes.

There's a deadness inside of me that emerges strong. It spreads like black night over Martha and the room and keeps my hands clutched tight around her neck until finally she gives in. Her body goes limp.

I let go and step back feeling a wicked smile broaden my face. I tie the string around her wrist and make sure the bell is securely positioned.

She will live if the mortuary wants her to. All she has to do is breathe. Fight for her life like I had to.

I step from the room and sit down in the chair outside the mortuary window. I watch and wait until the late beams of afternoon light push through the broken window from the other side of the room and remind me to go home.

Chapter Fifteen

"*Casey, get up!*"

My heart jumpstarts.

"What's wrong with you?" Kenny asks, shaking my arm.

For a second, I'm not sure if I'm awake or dreaming but with each one of his shakes I feel like I'm coming back into my body. I struggle to roll over and sit up. A thin trickle of drool leaks from my mouth.

Kenny grabs the water bottle from the side of the bed and unscrews the top. "Here, drink this."

I try and raise a shaky arm. It feels like a weight is attached to it. I take a drink. My stomach clenches.

"You need to get to a doctor," he says. His voice echoes. I'm going to go call someone."

"Please don't leave me alone."

With every breath it feels like I can't get enough air in my lungs. I take another drink. I run a hand through my hair feeling the dampness and turn to look behind at my pillow, soaked with sweat and vomit. Bits of white pills scatter the sheets.

He calls the hospital, nervously glancing to me every other word as he says, "Shaky. Pale. Yellow eyes."

Yellow eyes? I force myself to look over at my bedside mirror. My eyes strain to make out my blurry image. Even from several feet away I can see how sick I am. I flop back down to the bed, my head spinning.

"I'll bring her in right away," Kenny says as he lowers the phone. "Okay, let's go."

He forces me to stand. With every step, I feel my legs wobble. As we head out of the room, I can't help but notice my bedroom door, the frame cracked, the lock broken. My stomach heaves as I feel like I'm going to be sick again. I turn away from Kenny and throw up the water I just drank along with more pills.

When I turn back around, Kenny's face pales.

"Y-you're going to be all right," he says again, but even as sick as I am, I can make out the noticeable tone of doubt in his voice.

It takes us a good five minutes to get down the stairs.

Kenny's arm strains against the railing as he tries to keep us both from tumbling headfirst. Once downstairs, he steadies me against the wall and bangs on Martha's bedroom door, twists the door handle, and yells out, "Martha! We've got kind of an emergency here. You think you could help?"

The noise he's making reverberates in my head. I clutch my ears.

When she doesn't answer, Kenny rushes back to my side and gets me to the garage door. "Stay here," he orders.

He goes into Martha's room and then returns. "She's not here. Damn it, she's finally gone. Whatever. Come on. I can get you there myself."

"You're going to drive?"

"I can do it. I've practiced a bunch."

Kenny gets me outside and into the car. As he drives, his eyes dart to me and then the road. He brakes hard at one point nearly colliding with a parked car.

My stomach twists. There's an ache in my back and chest. I feel like I'm going to hurl. "Lower the window," I beg him.

The cool evening air brushes against my skin and turns my hot sweat cold.

"You're going to be okay," Kenny says in a reassuring tone. "You're just sick."

He's right. I feel sick inside and outside. My soul feels sick. Every person on the street points an accusing finger at me. The dog in the car beside us growls and bares his teeth at me. The red light takes forever as the animal goes mad tearing at the window as if to break it and rip out my throat. I'm a mistake. A tragic mistake. I should've died in Phish's torture chamber. Now, I'm nothing more than a festering pustule of sickness.

"Hold on, Casey." Kenny grabs my arm. "Two minutes."

I lean back against the headrest. The dizziness makes me feel as if the car is spinning. I try and focus but it's no use.

"We're here." Kenny stops the car.

The door opens and slams shut. A moment later, my door opens and a gush of air blows over me.

"She looks bad," a voice says.

My eyes feel sealed shut, but I force them open to see a large man in a white uniform lifting me out of the car.

"Kenny," I mutter.

The man ignores me. A moment later I'm on a gurney. Another man appears. Together, they push me out of the evening air and into the bright, white lights of the hospital.

I feel myself whisked away. My clothes are stripped from my body. A hospital gown is put on. There are IVs in my arms. "I-I need something," I say to the nurse who passes by.

Again, more words coming from me and at me. I'm in a tunnel. Their words are hollow. A clear tube appears.

"This might hurt, honey," says someone and I feel it pushed into my nose.

I gag and fight it off, but she holds my arms. My eyes water. The lights above me dance and I begin to feel a fade to black, when someone shakes me back into reality. A cool sensation hits my center. I heave again feeling every ounce of my stomach come unglued and empty into the tube.

"Relax, dear," the woman says.

But it's impossible. Again, my stomach clenches. The poison is pulled from me. I try and laugh, tears stream down my cheeks as I think they're going to need a stronger tool to get all of the poison out of my veins, where it's seeped into every cell and ounce of my DNA. When they finally pull the tube out and release my arms, my hands fly to my throat as I try to soothe the pain in my esophagus.

"Enough," I manage to say. "Get away from me."

"We just saved your life," the nurse says, checking my vitals.

I point to Phish, standing behind her. "Get him away from me."

She turns to follow my gaze. When she turns to face me, I see it in her eyes. She knows something.

Thoughts fly through my head of Devin Phish. "He's watching me," I mutter as I twist back and forth sure every orderly that passes is another version of him.

"You're all right," the nurse says. "I'll get the doctor."

I try to sit up. It feels too familiar here and I begin to think I've been taken back to the hospital where I fought for my life, where I killed Phish in the morgue downstairs, the worst hospital in the whole area. I'm back at Bridgeport Hospital.

In every shadow Phish lurks. Every EMT that whisks past me is a serial killer ready to take me out. I twist back and forth in bed. Blood trickles down my arm as the needle comes loose. I need to get out of here.

"Hold on there," a man's voice says.

I struggle to get a good look at him. White coat. Doctor.

"What medications are you on?" he asks.

My mouth moves, but I'm not sure if words are coming out.

His pen clicks.

"Don't let him take me," I say as Phish's sinister face appears over the doctor's shoulder.

The doctor calls out for a medication, a long chemical name that's beyond my grasp as I try to fight off the smell of decayed breath. Again, I twist in the bed as Phish leans closer.

"Better not do that," the doctor warns me to stop fighting the IV.

"Do we need security?" the nurse asks.

"She'll be okay," he says as he injects something into the bag.

The pain from the last few hours begins to pull back. The dull, constant ache in my head withdraws along with the blurry waves and murmuring voices. Phish pulls back to the corner.

The doctor's light shines again in my eyes as I wince. He begins to say something when a loud screech interrupts him and I wish for the silence again.

"Shotgun victim," another voice yells out.

The nurse sighs. "Busy night. It never ends, does it?"

Someone pulls the white curtain at my side only I can see clearly around it and the rush of caregivers flooding toward the emergency entrance. I can't be here.

Voices yell out orders. There are too many of them. They overlap each other and their hands are blurs as they work to save the man's life.

I struggle to take out the IV. Blood splatters onto my gown. I grab a bandage and wrap it tight then scan the messy scene for my clothes, finally finding them in a sealed bag at the end of the bed. I begin to change, shoving what feels like dead weight into each of the holes of my clothes, yanking up my jeans then forcing my two lifeless arms into the sleeves.

"Hey, what are you doing?" the nurse yells at me as she holds the shotgun victim's arms. "Get back in bed." The nurse shouts for security but they're consumed by the next patient flying through the door.

I grab my shoes and the plastic bag with my phone then hurry away from the chaotic scene and out the double doors.

Only the doors don't lead back to the entrance like I thought they would. Instead, I'm inside the hospital. The hallways are cold. I trace the walls with one hand, steading myself every few feet. The sick smell of alcohol surrounds me. My legs tremble. I search for an exit only everything feels blurred. With each step, I tell myself I'm closer to getting out of this place. I have to leave before something worse happens.

At the end of every hallway there's another turn or corridor that leads to a stairwell with locked doors and a place for a badge swipe. I go down another level and try the door, but it's locked again, only I pull at it a couple times to make sure, and bang until the echoes fill the stairwell.

A man from above calls down, “What’s going on?”

“I’m stuck,” I shout up.

“Use your swipe card,” he says. “Wait, who are you?”

Ignoring him, I continue to descend to the next level until I realize this is the last door. When it doesn’t open, I lean to the side and try to focus on what I’m going to do. The lights are barely strong enough to see my way back upstairs. Styrofoam cups and cigarette butts lay propped in corners with the heavy smell of something more chemical lingering all around me.

I dig my phone out of the plastic bag and text Kenny that I’ve left the emergency room only there’s no signal. Not in the bottom of this building. Probably nowhere in the hospital.

Just as I’m about to return to the stairs, the door in front of me opens. A man in a white uniform comes out. I quickly turn and rush through the opening and into what I’m pretty sure is the basement of Bridgeport Hospital.

My spine stiffens as I pass the shrouded bodies. The scent of formaldehyde is in the air, reminding me of the waiting mortuary. A stronger smell clings to the walls and ceiling. I know it too well. Death and decay surround me as I realize I’ve found my way, once again, to the morgue. Memories of being here before flood my mind. Phish brought me here. He shoved me in one of the morgue fridges inside a body bag until I fought my way out and fought him to death.

I just need a way out, an exit. The air feels colder in one direction. It must be where they bring in the bodies. I rush toward it, feeling the sting of a sharp headache begin, which is only slightly more intense than the soreness in my throat from the tube.

As I near the exit, a large open garage door, I spot a man standing there. He leans against the wall smoking.

Only he separates me from the dark night outside. I wait for what feels like eternity for him to finish his smoke and leave, but he doesn't.

Finally, I stand and inch my way closer, ready to run past him if I need to.

He finishes his cigarette and flicks it outside, then turns to face me just as I'm about to make my mad escape.

"Casey," he says, stopping me. "What are you doing here?"

Chapter Sixteen

L*ance's head flinches back slightly.*

His dark hair blows gently in the wind coming through the wide door behind him, framing the bewildered look on his face.

My arms cross as he lets me go. "*What am I doing here*?" I ask. "What are *you* doing here?"

His eyes go to the hospital bracelet around my wrist.

I avert my gaze. I feel my ears turn red. Nothing could be worse than letting him see me like this, but then I scan his clothes. He's dressed head to toe in a black Bridgeport Hospital uniform.

His hands go to my shoulders as he steadies me. When he reaches a hand to my chin, I can feel his warm fingertips on my cold skin, but still I pull away.

"Let me take you back inside," he says.

"You're an employee?" I whisper. "In the morgue? Am I some kind of sick joke to you?"

"There's nothing funny about this," he says. "Let me help you back inside."

"No." I swat away his hand. "I can't go back in there."

"You need to lie down." He points to my sleeve where blood has soaked through the bandage. "Let me take care of you."

I don't budge. My mind spins as I try to make sense of why he's lied to me again. Aunt Martha's words reappear as I begin to wonder if there's more he's not telling me.

Lance sighs. His hands drop. "I wanted to tell you about this job," he says. "I just didn't want to upset you."

"You work in the same morgue that Phish used to dump his torture victims. How could you not tell me?"

At first his face is blank and then he says, "I needed a job."

I feel so used. This on top of him lying about where he lives. I'm at a loss for words until finally I say, "Did you know Devin Phish? Were you in on it?"

His eyes widen. "Are you kidding me?"

"What other reason is there for how you appeared the other night near my car? You were waiting for me. You're a serial killer junky, aren't you? Maybe you're just trying to see if you can retraumatize his victim."

"Stop it," Lance says. "You couldn't be further from the truth."

"Then, what's the truth?" I demand.

"I got hired working in the morgue after I dropped out of school. There weren't too many places hiring seventeen-year-old kids without a diploma. I just help out, okay?"

I can only imagine how he helps out. Carrying in body bags, transporting the deceased to mortuaries. It's everything I'm trying to get away from. It suddenly dawns on me that Lance is just another player sent to remind me that I can never be free of my past. "And, I thought you were trying to help me. You really are sick and twisted, you know that?"

"Me?" he laughs and steps closer. "What about you?

Did you kill that girl they found chopped up in the park? The one you were talking about all night?"

At first, I ignore his question. I owe him nothing. Then I say, "Did you?"

"What's that supposed to mean?" he asks.

"You had just as much opportunity to kill Ally Parker as I did. At some point that evening we separated. How do I know you didn't run off to kill her?"

He stops and stares hard at me, then finally he opens his mouth and says, "Fine. You caught me. I did it."

"What?"

"Yeah." He runs a hand through his hair and steps closer. "I dropped you at your house and used your car to go to the park where you said she plays tennis."

My eyes widen.

"She was there, and I thought to myself, why does a girl like that get everything while you get screwed. It should've been her, not you, so I took her, chopped her up, and left her there."

"And, the finger?" I ask, my voice wavering.

He raises a brow. "What finger?"

I shudder, unsure if he's going to hurt me, too.

Instead, he steps back and sends me a long, pained look. "You need to relax," he whispers.

"Are you lying to me, *again*?"

"Of course," he says. "How could you think I'd do something like that?"

The pain of the overdose still throbs in my head as I try to massage it away. All of this is too much and I need to get away from him.

"You suspect the worst in everyone, don't you? Even me. I'm not a killer, Casey. I care about you. Stop imagining the worst. You can trust me."

"Trust you?" I say, feeling even more betrayed than

moments before. "You lied about this job, where you live, killing Ally, and your parents. Did you kill them?" It's a low blow.

His face turns serious as I sputter, "N-never mind. It doesn't matter. None of this matters." I push past him.

His hand brushes against mine as he tries to hold on to it. "Where are you going?"

"Home," I say.

"How?"

"I'll walk."

"Wait," Lance calls out. "You can't walk back to Westport. It's miles away. You'd have to cross the bridge, and it's freezing out there. Listen, give me a second. I'll find you a ride."

But, spending another second in this hospital isn't going to happen. I turn and rush out the docking door willing to take my chances. My thoughts run rampant as I rush away from him.

Outside, the weather's turned icy cold, winter like. Stark tree branches reach for the night's sky, illuminated by passing headlights and the pulsing flash of police cars. Old Bridgeport brick buildings line the streets in every direction. Only a few storefronts are lit. Most have metal shutters spray painted with graffiti. The air has the scent of diesel mixed with snow. I clutch my sweater tighter, wishing I would've worn my coat into the hospital.

The road down from the facility leads to Bridgeport Bridge. I can spot it in the distance, lit up with white light. I've seen it a dozen times before. All I have to do is get there, cross over to Westport.

The ache throbs in my head. The cold air stings my lungs but wakes me to my surroundings. I try to stay focused on the bridge. It's hard to ignore every dark alley that I pass and the feeling that maybe I made a mistake not taking Lance up on his offer to find me a ride.

How could I have been so naïve? I let someone in my life, and he betrays me with a scattering of lies within the first few days. I can't help but wonder if this will be the pattern for the rest of my life. Will I always trust the wrong people? Am I doomed to be alone? And, the worst of it is there's no such thing as being truly alone for me, not with the haunts of Phish, Grandmother, and now Ally lingering nearby.

Twenty minutes pass when I begin to lose feeling in my toes. My fingertips ache no matter how many times I slap them against my legs. I scratch my head and look around to hitch a ride. I put out my thumb the best I can for the next car that passes.

A car slows. Its headlights flash onto my face as I try and shield my eyes from its glare. In the driver's seat is a man. He takes one look at me and speeds up.

The next three cars do the same.

I remember my yellow eyes, the blood soaking through my sweater, and the hospital band around my wrist. I twist at it to pull it off, but the plastic won't relent, and I keep moving. Ten more minutes, I tell myself. The bridge looms larger but with every step it seems I'm unable to reach it.

Lance was right. It will take forever to get back. My feet begin to feel numb and I stumble. My head clouds as I see ambulances race past me and a few more cars, then a police car which jars me awake.

Behind me, Lance's voice calls out again. I take a deep breath, pull back against the wall of an old building, and press myself against the cold, hard brick. It's no use trying to talk to him. Not after the lies.

Above me the clouds are heavy against the full moon. The streets are nearly empty and only a few cars go past.

There's no way I can stop. I'll freeze to death out here. I force my legs to move. I have to get to the bridge that separates this nightmarish side of town from my home.

Up ahead, a couple just coming off the bridge glance toward me and hurry past.

The wind blows hard off the river, pushing up from below. It pierces through my skin and burns my lungs as I step onto the crossway. My hands fly to my mouth. I take short, fast breaths into my balled-up fists and try to get some circulation. When I finally reach the top, I gaze down to the water below.

The dark river moves fast like my thoughts. I keep walking. Phish did his best to kill me. But he lost. Aunt Martha did her best to scare me. I won't let her win. With every step it becomes clearer. I must stay alive. There's every reason in the world to give up, but I won't.

My thoughts turn to Kenny. He rescued me from myself. I can't let him down. From deep within, I search for the strength that I had to survive Devin Phish. It's in there and I have to rekindle it. Not many people can say they survived a serial killer. Fewer can say they found a way to overcome the trauma of it, but I will. For myself and for Kenny.

I fight across the bridge to the safety of Westport. Tomorrow, I vow, I will talk to the detectives. With every ounce of strength that I can gather, I force my feet to move as I take one last step off the bridge. The stars above spin. My head goes numb as I collapse to the side of the road.

Chapter Seventeen

"*Wake up.*"

His voice comes from somewhere above.

I feel his hands around my waist.

My body is weightless as he lifts me from the cold, hard pavement to somewhere inside where there's more light and a scent of something freshly baked. The warmth brings me to my senses. My eyes flutter open.

"Come on," he says. "Sit down. Let me get you something hot to drink."

"Leave me alone," I say as I ease myself into a chair.

Lance rushes to the counter where a concerned looking man wearing a white apron nods and begins steaming something.

"Where am I?" I ask when Lance returns to the table.

He pulls off his coat and drapes it around my shoulders. "Coffee shop," he says. "The man behind the counter is the one who found you on the sidewalk. I would never have found you if I didn't hear him yelling."

I fidget in my chair as I pull Lance's coat tighter.

The man from behind the counter puts a cup in front of me. "Drink this," he says. "It will help you."

"Thank you," I say as I bring the warm liquid to my lips and sip. It heats my mouth and coats the stinging pain in my throat. For a second I think I might throw it back up, but my stomach gurgles and warmth begins to spread out from my center.

"Are you all right?" the man asks.

I slowly nod and take another sip. "I didn't know it would be so cold tonight."

"Seasons change fast around here," he says. "Snow's coming. You just rest. Let me know if you need anything."

My hands stay glued to the sides of the cup as I raise it again to my lips.

"I can't believe you tried to walk," Lance says. His hand taps nervously against the table. "You could've died out there."

"Why didn't you let me die?" I whisper. "You seem to get off on death."

"You know why," he says. His eyes grow larger as he whispers, "We need each other."

It feels inevitable. We always seem to find one another. In a way, it comforts me to be needed. But also, it feels sick. Nothing could be worse than being needed and followed by a liar.

"On the sidewalk," Lance says. "Geez, Casey. You would've frozen in the night."

I can't argue with him. I slowly lower the cup. "I guess it was stupid. Impulsive to run."

"Why did you do it then?"

"The hospital," I say. "I'm never going back there. It's where they took me after the waiting mortuary. It's where I killed Phish. I'll never be a patient at Bridgeport Hospital again."

"Okay, but what about a different hospital? Maybe a private doctor to look you over."

"I'm better now," I say. "I don't need a doctor. I know what I'm doing. I can figure this out on my own."

His forehead wrinkles, but I won't change my mind. "I haven't been able to trust a lot of people, either," he says. "I'm alone a lot too, but you've got to take help from someone. What you've been through—"

"Is none of your business," I say.

He leans back in his chair. His eyes search mine. "You've got to let me explain."

Taking another sip of the drink, I say, "It's not necessary. I don't really care why you lied about everything. I was quick to trust you. I won't make that mistake again."

His hand sneaks across the table. He places it on top of mine. "If you'd just listen—"

I pull back. "You already told me. You took the job because you needed money." I sit there stone cold.

Lance's face pales. "You won't let me explain?"

"Why did you make up living in that apartment?"

He fidgets with the end of his scarf.

My anger spikes. "Tell me the truth," I demand. "Where do you—"

"Nowhere," he says, raising his gaze to me. "I've been staying in one of the open units. I go there sometimes to get away from everything. There are a few furnished ones and they're a lot better than wandering the streets."

"Did you run away from your foster family?"

"I'm eighteen in two months," he says. "No one cares."

"Maybe the police do," I say.

"Casey, look around. This side of town is safe, but where you just came from, that side of town, *Bridgeport*, is teeming with problems—big problems. The cops don't care about some seventeen-year-old trying to live on his own, okay?"

He's right about that. I think for a second about myself. How in just a few months I'll be eighteen, too, and if Aunt Martha is really gone what it will mean for me and worse, what it will mean for Kenny who's got another year and half.

"My brother," I say, fumbling for my phone. "I have to text him and tell him I'm okay."

Before Lance can say anything else, I quickly send Kenny a message then lean back and rub my temples. Deep in my bones I feel tired. There's a part of me that feels older, too. If only I could find peace.

"I don't know what I'm going to do," I say. "I'm trying so hard to get past what happened last summer. The medication my doctor gave me doesn't seem to help and no matter how hard I try to deal with my feelings, the fear, anger, worry, I can't seem to move past them to something better."

"What is it you want?" he asks.

"To be healed," I say.

Lance reaches for me again. "It takes time."

"I went back to the waiting mortuary to deal with the past. I dealt with it. Now what?"

"Now, you move forward."

"But how? It still feels as if I'm chained to what happened. Why can't I let this go?"

"We can help each other," Lance says, brushing his finger against mine. His long bang covers his eye. He swings it back and I can see how sincere he is about moving forward, needing me, and I can't help but wonder if I need him just as much.

There's still uncertainty there. I pull one hand back and rub my chin as I gather the courage to ask about his parents, the accident, and all the horrible things Aunt Martha said, but I don't because for a split second I feel something I haven't felt in a long time, maybe never, but it's there like the lightest breath of fresh air.

Lance's gaze fills me with hope.

It's more care and concern than I've felt in my entire life from anyone. It makes it hard to breathe because I suddenly know why he came after me and didn't let me freeze to death on the street. I know why he's fighting for us now. He needs me and I need him just as much. He won't let go of us and I need his strength, so I don't ask him to explain himself. I let his past be a secret if it means keeping what we have right now in this moment.

That's the problem with being a broken person. We have to survive. Somehow, we have to fit our shattered pieces together to make ourselves whole. And, somehow it has to be good enough.

I flip my hand, palm up, and let the warmth of his touch renew me. His lies are not unlike my own but the two us, from such chaos, how will we ever find what's whole?

Chapter Eighteen

I *finish the last sip of the warm drink.*

"I'll call someone to get you back home," Lance says.

"It's fine," I say, handing back his coat. "I think I can walk the rest of the way."

Those words seem to trigger the man behind the counter who comes to the table and says, "No, you can't walk. It's much too cold out there. Take a taxi."

I shake my head. "I don't have any money."

His eyes flash to the dried blood on my arm. "Hold on." He rushes to the counter and a few seconds later stuffs a few dollars into my hands. "It's not safe to walk, especially in your condition."

My heart warms at his kindness. I'm not used to it and tears begin to spring out of nowhere. "Thank you," is all I can muster as I slowly stand and leave.

Outside, Lance waves down a cab and we get in. The car's heater blows strong, hot air on the both of us as I give the directions to the driver and sit back, thinking of Kenny and worried that he still hasn't texted me back.

"It's probably the reception," Lance says. "A lot of the messages don't go through."

Still, I quickly send him another text to come back home. Everything is fine.

At the house, Lance and I walk up the front path. The front door is slightly open, and I can't remember in all the chaos how Kenny and I left the house.

"I don't think your aunt would like it if she knew I was here," he says.

"She left," I say as I press the door closed. I go to the guest room and look inside. Every piece of what Martha came with is gone. The closets are empty. Only a few things remain in the bathroom.

"I guess it's for good," I say.

"Mind if I crash on the couch?" he asks.

"You can sleep in here tonight," I say. "Just let me change the sheets."

I walk to the closet, noticing the alarm clock beside the guest bed that says it's after one o'clock. My head and body feel heavy as I pull off the old sheets and toss them in the corner.

Lance slowly takes off his jacket, while I shove all the dirty laundry into the washing machine and head upstairs.

Inside Kenny's room, his bed is made. He hasn't been back since the hospital.

As I make my way to my room, I see the broken doorframe. I slide my hand along the edges and take in the damage. The lock is broken, and the frame cracked. As I step inside, I sense the change. It's no longer my sanctuary. The disturbed energy of my torment is there. What's left of the pills I took lay scattered on the nightstand. I flick off the light and slowly step out.

"No one is here," I say to Lance. "Should I go back to the hospital to look for Kenny?"

"I don't think that's a good idea," he says. "What if he's on his way back here?"

Lance is right. We'd just keep passing each other if I tried to make my way back there and without a car or money it wouldn't be easy. Instead, I make a quick call to the Bridgeport Hospital and leave a message for them to check the waiting room and notify Kenny to return home immediately.

The woman who answers isn't the friendliest, but she finally agrees to tell him right before hanging up on me.

"Maybe we should get some rest," Lance says. "It's late."

He's right. Exhaustion and the night's events have worn me down. There's still a dull ache in the back of my head from the pills. If only I could take something else to make it go away, but I decide that I've had enough of medications for the night. I quickly make up the guest bed.

"I'm going to sleep on the couch," I say. "I need to be here when my stepbrother gets back."

"You should take the bed," he says.

"It's fine," I say, grateful to have him there. His presence is warming to my harsh experiences of the last few nights. I slowly close the bedroom door and make my way to the couch.

There's so much going through my head when it comes to Lance. One minute he fills me with hope. I want nothing more than for him to be with me and in the next minute I'm not sure if I've made a good decision. If I've somehow invited an unstable, not completely honest guy into my life without really knowing anything about him.

It's in times like this I wish I had someone older and wiser to talk to. I reach for my bracelet, but remember it's gone, and Mother is not likely to answer my call even if I tried.

With a throw pillow and blanket covering me, I feel the heaviness of sleep begin to quiet my thoughts. It's been a long day. My body aches from what I've put it through. My throat still feels sore. Taking those pills was just about the dumbest thing I could've done and for what?

Running away was not the answer. I have to talk to the police and straighten everything out and with Lance there to support me we'll settle this quickly. A part of me regrets terrifying Kenny like that. I can only imagine the worry I put him through. The only thing I ever wanted was to shield him from the world and I brought the worst of it straight to him.

I rub my forehead and try to let go of my mistakes from the day. Forgiveness has never been my strongest suit, but if I'm ever going to move forward, I'm going to have to learn to forgive myself. My only hope is that Kenny sees it the same way I do and doesn't flinch at the sight of me when he comes home.

My eyelids close as the weight of sleep sinks in. For the first times in months, I don't dream, and when I wake there's a soft hue of sunlight warming my face and a chill in the air.

I push myself up only to find the front door wide open and the cold morning air causing the heating system to work overtime. I stand and close it, wondering if Kenny came home while I slept. I rush upstairs to find his bed is still empty.

Back at the couch, I fish through the cushions to find my phone. A new text. I click on it and read, "Just got all your messages. Be back soon."

I breathe a sigh of relief. Finally, Kenny's on his way home.

I wrap the blanket tighter around myself and shuffle to the kitchen, feeling hungrier than I've been in weeks. With

Martha gone and her nasty energy cleared out of the house, everything feels somehow lighter and in a weird way, with Lance asleep in the adjacent room, and the house all to ourselves, it feels more like home, like family. I decide to make a good breakfast with the remaining sandwich bread and whatever's left in the fridge, which ends up being one orange and two slices of ham, and a tiny bit of butter. It will have to do.

As the bread toasts, I begin to wonder if Martha was serious yesterday about calling the police. As far as I know they never came to the house. I remember her going for her phone. I question if she was really calling my parents instead of the police to tell them she was leaving.

The toaster pops, and I gather the food onto a tray and bring it to Lance.

He sleeps soundly in the guest bed. His slow, deep breaths make me want to curl around him and sleep a while longer. I put the tray on the side table.

Lance stirs. "What's that?" he asks, sitting up.

"It's for you," I say, easing to his side.

"I should be the one making you breakfast." He reaches for his t-shirt, but not before I take in his smooth chest and muscly arms.

He catches my eyes and puts the shirt down.

I snuggle into his chest. There's no better feeling than being this close to him. I raise my chin and let him kiss me. In those moments, it feels like the old, dark world of my past begins to crumble. Towers of old memories and grudges shift in their foundations.

When I pull back, I can feel the rapid pulse of my heart. His warm breath and strong hands send me into overdrive. If only it could be like this forever.

"This is what I figure," I say, taking a breath. "We both

haven't started out being a hundred percent honest with each other. I guess getting to know someone can be hard. I want to start again, only this time I want us to be honest with each other."

I stand and hand him the plate of food.

He takes it. "I promise to be honest with you as long as you promise to ask for help if you need it."

I press my lips together. My heart skips a beat because I think about not ever feeling the protection I feel from him and how badly I've always needed it. I sink into his chest again and lay my head there. His warmth and the sound of his steady heart centers me.

After a minute, I push up and say, "I will," knowing Lance is my center. He will protect me. "I have to talk to the detectives today. Will you help me?"

He nods and a wave of relief washes over me. "I have to change first."

As I make my way back upstairs to the bathroom, I can't help but finally feel some peace that I deserve. I flinch at how close I came to losing everything in one night, and how far I've come in dealing with my fears. I quickly get ready, but the feeling of hospital funk is still all over me and I'm in desperate need of a shower. I peel off my previous day's clothes and take a look at myself again in the mirror, still not a hundred percent satisfied with what peers back, but I shrug it off.

My eyes are back to normal. The wound from the IV and the ache in my throat from the tube still hurt. Once showered and changed, I head back downstairs to the sound of the front door opening and closing.

"Kenny?" I call out.

Only when I get to the bottom, it's not Kenny standing there.

Two detectives wait in the front hallway, one with her badge displayed clearly on her jacket.

"Casey McClair?" she says. "We have a few questions for you."

Chapter Nineteen

"*How did you get in here?*"

"Your door was open," the female detective says. "I think the lock is broken." Her dark brown eyes and hair work to only strengthen her already sharp features. Something about her rattles me. I get the feeling like I've seen her before.

I pull the towel from my head. "The lock might be broken," I say as I come into the living room. "But that doesn't give you the right to come into my house."

"We were concerned," the second detective says. He's taller than anyone I know. His presence makes my jaw tighten as he strides closer, but there's also something soothing in his soft gaze. "Are you home alone, Casey?"

My eyes flash behind me. "No," I say. "My boyfriend is here." I can hardly believe I just called Lance my boyfriend and out loud before discussing it with him, but it's too late now. I go to the guest bedroom as the detectives follow, close on my heels.

Inside, the bed is empty. The sheets lay in a clump on the ground. I turn my eyes to the adjacent bathroom. The light is off, and a sinking feeling begins to come over me as I realize he's gone.

When I slowly turn to face the detectives, I feel rattled but not enough to give up. I'll face this fear, too, just like the others.

"I guess I am alone," I say.

They back up to let me slide by. "We'd just like to ask you some questions," the man says.

"Here?" I ask, threading my fingers through my hair. "I mean do you want me to go down to the station?"

"Not just yet," she says. "Do you want to sit?"

I slowly nod and together we go back into the living room. I settle back into the same spot where I slept while they sit beside each other on the opposite couch.

"I'm Detective Sanchez," the woman says. "And this is Detective Connor."

"Is there an adult you can call to be here?" Detective Connor asks.

"My Aunt Martha is usually here," I say. "She may have just gone out for a bit." A small lie, but necessary.

"Normally, we wait for an adult to return," he says, "But in this case, we're here just to find out some information."

I take a slow breath. That's a good sign. I try to relax and not think about how Lance ditched me. Right when I needed him to give me an alibi and he leaves.

"Are you sick?" Detective Sanchez asks.

"No," I say. "Why would you ask that?"

She points to the needle mark on my arm.

I cover it with my towel. "Oh, that. I was in the hospital last night."

The detectives glance to one another as Sanchez pulls a pad of paper from her pocket and begins. "We don't want to rattle you, Casey," she says. "I know what you went through this past summer."

It suddenly registers where I know her from. "You were there. In the hospital."

"I was the detective assigned to your case," she says. "I saw you on the day of your rescue."

My head slowly nods.

"What you went through with Devin Phish was terrible," she says. "No one, especially someone your age should ever have to suffer that way."

"Thanks, I guess," I say, not knowing how to respond when I'm not sure what she'll ask next.

Detective Connor leans closer. "I'm not supposed to say this, but I'm glad you killed him."

My eyes widen and Detective Sanchez clears her throat.

"We're not really here about that," she says. "With the cooperation of our other key witness, Sebastian Trawler, we were able to confirm what happened at Kessler's Funeral Home. With his statements the property was condemned. The case was closed unless there are more bodies discovered that can somehow be linked to Devin Phish."

Her words somehow jar the memory of the boy, Sebastian, and I remember him standing there in the living room of the waiting mortuary with another man. I lower my head. My eyes shift back and forth as I try to remember his name, then I look up.

"What is it?" Detective Connor asks.

"The mortuary," I say. "That old man who kept me there, what was his name?"

"Alfred Kessler," he says. "He ran Kessler's Funeral Home for years. He was always a little eccentric, but after his wife died it became too hard for him. Poor man killed himself in the house."

My breath catches. I think back to the splatters of blood in one of the bedrooms of the house, the flashing eyes in the mortuary, and the sound the chair made as if someone was sitting down to watch another victim on the table fight between life and death. I can't help but wonder if his spirit is still somehow in that house.

"But he wasn't a murderer, right?" I ask.

"No," Detective Connor says. "He was used by Devin Phish to help get rid of the bodies. He never killed anyone. At least, not intentionally."

I can't help but wonder if Alfred Kessler's ghost is still tormented by what he witnessed. If he needs help, too.

"Casey?" Detective Sanchez says, pulling me back around. "You okay?"

"I'm fine," I say. "I never met Sebastian," I say. "I only saw him a little bit in school before I was kidnapped and maybe for a moment the night of my rescue. I never saw him after that and I'm not attending classes anymore. At least not for now."

Detective Connor nods. Our eyes meet and there's something in his expression like he wants to say more but before he can Detective Sanchez says, "We'll try and make this quick." She clicks her pen. Her eyes focus on me like she's preparing to gauge my response. "We have to ask about your connection to Ally Parker."

"I-I have no connection to her," I say. "I mean last summer she trained me for the tennis team. You know that, don't you? I was kidnapped after one of our lessons."

"Sure," Detective Connor says. "Yeah, we know she helped you—"

"It's awful what happened to her," I interrupt.

Detective Sanchez shifts on the couch. "I would

imagine you'd feel that way. It's a lot like what happened to you."

"I didn't get cut up," I say. "I fought back. I defended myself. I didn't get killed. I had to do it. I'm not a victim."

There's a moment of silence like someone stopped to take a picture. Each of us sits there, frozen from my outburst. I press my eyes closed, wishing for the calming buzz of one of Dr. Bruner's pills, and then I try again. "I'm sorry," I say, returning my gaze to them. "I've just been through a lot and I'm trying to get better. This might be too much right now."

"We know, Casey," Detective Connor says. "Maybe we should come back when your Aunt returns."

Nothing would give me more relief than for them to go and leave me alone but then they'll be back and who knows when and I need for this to be over, so before Detective Sanchez can put away her notepad, I say, "I didn't go to the park that day."

She nods. "Her friends say you were at the park a lot, maybe following Ally."

"I did follow her," I admit. "But only at the park. I went to watch her play." I don't let them know all the other thoughts. How I wanted to see her suffer instead of me. How I wished her dead, but I feel like they already know that, too, and I begin to wonder if detectives are trained mind readers. If it's somehow a requirement of their job.

"Is that the only reason you went to the park?" Detective Connor asks.

"I didn't do anything," I say. "I have an alibi for the night she disappeared."

Detective Sanchez leans in. "What is it?"

"I was with my boyfriend," I say. "All night."

"And what's his name?" she asks.

"Lance," I whisper, eyeing the guest bedroom, half believing he's hiding in there. "Lance Crux."

Again, the detectives glance at each other. The name must be familiar. If Martha knew him, there's no doubt the detectives do too, but I don't want to find out if he's as awful as Martha said. I don't want them to tell me he was a suspect in his parents' murder, a runaway, a liar, or worse.

"And where were … the two of you?" Detective Connor asks.

I cross my hands in my lap. If I'm going to rid myself of my worry, I have to come clean about it. "I went back to the waiting mortuary. I mean Kessler's Funeral Home."

"Why?" Detective Sanchez asks, her eyes narrowing.

"It's something I'm working on," I say. "I'm dealing with confronting the past."

Detective Connor clucks his tongue. "Just my two cents, kid, but I don't think you should go back to that house. They're tearing the whole block down. It's not safe."

"It's also trespassing," Detective Sanchez says.

I slowly nod. "I just wanted to see it during the daylight."

She writes something else in her notepad.

The sting of last night's headache returns. "Is there anything else?" I ask. "I'm not really feeling up to more questions."

"No," Detective Connor says. "I think that's all we need."

Detective Sanchez doesn't look as sure but finally she stands, and they walk to the door. "We'll need you to not go too far," she says. "It could be safer for you to stay home. At least until we have a better idea on who took Ally Parker."

A part of me agrees with her, but it won't be in my

bedroom. I decide right then and there to turn the guest bedroom into my new sanctuary.

As they step outside, I spot a car in the driveway. *My car* and Kenny in the driver's seat. The detectives pass him as he steps out. His face lights up when he sees me. He rushes up the walk. "Where have you been?" he asks.

"*Where have I been*?" I hug him tight. "I texted and called you."

"I didn't get anything," he says. "I was sitting in the waiting room all night for news about you and then when I finally got up the nerve to ask this morning, they said you went home."

"What about the receptionist?" I ask. "Last night. Didn't she give you my message?"

He shakes his head and I practically kick the floorboard with anger about that stupid hospital and its inept workers.

"How are you feeling?" he asks, his eyes searching mine.

"I'm fine," I say. "Nothing to worry about. I'm just glad you're back."

He hugs me for a good minute and when he pulls away, we walk to the kitchen, past Martha's empty room.

"Where is she?" Kenny asks.

"Gone," I say. "But, listen we don't need her."

"She took all her stuff, huh?"

"Yes," I say as I go inside with him and gather the sheets.

"What's that?" He points to the tray on the nightstand.

"Breakfast," I say. "There's some stuff left in the fridge. I can make you something."

"Yeah. That would be great. I'm starving."

"Stay here." I quickly go to the kitchen and toast two more pieces of bread, then smear a pad of butter on each.

When I return, he's sitting on the bed with his head between his hands.

"Everything okay?" I ask and hand him the plate.

When he looks at me, he sighs and says, "Sure."

But I know what that tone means. He's stressing. "Don't worry," I say. "I'll get a job. Until Mom and Phil get back, we'll be okay."

Kenny blows out a quick breath. He puts the plate on the bed and runs his hands through his hair. "Casey, you're not well enough to get a job. You almost died last night."

"I made a mistake," I say. "A huge one. I shouldn't have put you in that position. I know it must have scared you, but I—"

"Enough," Kenny says. "I don't want to hear that you're better because I know you're not, not yet anyway. That's why we needed Martha. We needed her so that you could work on healing."

"But she wasn't helping me heal," I say. "She was making it worse for me."

"I know," he says. "I started to see that, too, but you still need to take care of yourself." He takes the laundry from me. "I'll start the wash, okay?"

"What about your toast?" I ask.

He returns and takes the plate in his other hand.

I feel as if some of the wind was knocked out of my sail. I wanted to show him everything was great again, but a part of me wonders what I can do now to repair the damage. There's only so much I can do to protect Kenny and being a mother figure to him feels hopelessly impossible when I can't even protect myself half the time.

"Maybe it was always supposed to be just the two of us," Kenny says as he turns in the doorway.

I can't help but wonder if he's right. After Lance's disappearing act, I start to think my strength is with my family and right now the only true family I've got is Kenny. I head to the bathroom to collect the used towels. One lays on the floor. Another is draped on the counter.

As I pull the hand towel from its holder the tinny sound of a ringing bell charges into me. I swallow as I realize behind the towel dangles a small bell, the same kind that hangs in the waiting mortuary. Its silver sides glisten as it shifts back and forth. The long, white string hangs down to the sink's edge. My tennis bracelet dangles there along with a note attached to the end. I draw up the string and read what it says. "*A souvenir for you.*" I flip over the note. On the back is a picture of Aunt Martha bound to one of the metal tables in the waiting mortuary.

Chapter Twenty

"*I think I'll stay home from school.*"

Kenny emerges from the laundry room and flicks on the television.

The blood drains from my face. A wave of nausea comes over me. I grip the towels tighter.

"You sure you're okay?" he asks. "Should we call Dr. Bruner?"

"No," I whisper. "I told you I made a huge mistake last night. I just need to rest. Do you mind watching upstairs?"

He yawns and stretches his arms over his head. "I probably should take a nap. Last night was crazy at that hospital. Do you know how many people came through there?"

I mask my worry until Kenny stops talking and finally disappears then drop the towels and rush to the bathroom. I lift the toilet lid and hang there for a minute. My stomach clenches. I'm not sure if it's from the charcoal from last night or seeing the picture of Aunt Martha strapped to one of the tables in the waiting mortuary. Either way, I feel the contents of my stomach come unglued. I curse Lance's name. It must have been him who left the bell for me to find. His idea of a sick joke. But why? Why would Lance want to torture me like this? I throw up again.

As I rock back on my heels and wipe my mouth, I feel the anger in my chest. I'll never trust him again. When I finally get up, I drink some water and grab my tennis bracelet, clasping it around my wrist. It's time for me to ask for help. I don't think I can go back to the waiting mortuary again. I decide to call my mother. Even if she refuses to come home, at least she'll know what to do. As I look for my phone, I hear behind me the newscaster on the television announcing the demolition of more homes in Bridgeport.

"Dozens of homes will be destroyed today," the reporter says as I slowly come around the corner to see the screen.

The camera flashes across a street I know too well and then a house I wish I never knew.

"Kessler's Funeral Home is scheduled for demolition today, but with the troubles the property faced this past summer, including a series of deaths and one suicide, there is some discussion of delay while the city continues its investigations."

I think of the bell hanging in the bathroom and the picture of Aunt Martha. If she is in the waiting mortuary, they'll destroy the house on top of her. I shove my phone in my bag. Once again, I quickly grab my coat and car keys. I have to get her out of there.

My hands shake as I try to clutch the steering wheel. I rifle through my bag and dig out one of the last of the pills I can manage to find. I can't help but remember promising Lance that I would ask for help if I needed it, but what about his promise to me? He said he would be there to help me with an alibi and then ditched me. I quickly pop the pill in my mouth and swallow.

Across town, I once again park my car outside Kessler's and get out.

I try to hurry inside as several people including cops wander nearby. A few neighbors further down lift what looks like a cabinet into a van. In the distance wrecking balls swing. It's hard to see but the smashing sound of metal on brick echoes around me and the smell of decades of dust filters through the wind.

I slowly head up the path and climb over the ledge. It's becoming too easy now. Only days before it terrified me to come this close.

Inside it's as dark as before.

I flick on my phone's flashlight and shine it on the floor ahead of me as I move past the kitchen and broken glass toward the back of the house. I want to call out to Aunt Martha, but my throat feels clamped shut and a part of me wants to believe that Lance is playing some kind of sick game, messing with my mind.

My eyes dart to the back of the room, to the same place where the darkened figure glared at me before. The watching chair still sits upright, the curtain is closed, and a sudden squeak makes me jump as the floorboards stir to life. Another rodent, as big as cat, scurries up the wall. My hands go wide. The rat looks back at me with red eyes. After another moment, it scurries across the ceiling, somehow clinging upside down, and then disappears into a hole in the upper corner of the room.

In the distance, there's a rumbling sound and crash. Another house gone, and soon this one, too. I pull back my shoulders and ease my way to the chair, waving a hand across the seat, half-expecting to feel something there.

When I don't feel anything, I push the chair to the ground and break off the last two legs. No one can sit in it now.

As I step back, I feel something tingle at my side. I turn to face it. There's nothing there, nothing I can see anyway, but a flurry of doubt lingers.

"I shouldn't be here," I say, bracing myself.

There's a sickening feeling in the pit of my stomach but I won't let it stop me. I drag back the curtain and it's as if I've been flung back into hell.

Chapter Twenty-One

A *rat chews on Aunt Martha's face.*

I scream and the rodent scurries away, but there are three other rats on the table that are not as easily scared off. My head feels woozy. Pressing a hand to the wall, I try to steady myself. I know I need help. Each time I look back, I see her mutilated body. The blood from her open wounds drips down to the floor. It's hard to get air into my lungs. I need to step away, but I need to help her.

Suddenly, Martha moans.

I glance up and watch as she slowly regains consciousness.

Her eyes open. She twists beneath her bondage and then stops when she sees me standing there, only a few feet away watching her through the mortuary window. Her gaze is fixed on me. She screams.

"Aunt Martha," I gasp.

Her mouth is stuffed with a rag and her muffled moans surround me.

"I'm going for help," I say.

She screams again and I can see she's bleeding horribly

now. The redness leaks from her legs and face where another rat has begun to gnaw away at her forehead.

My feet are two cement blocks. I can barely form words when there's a commotion at the front window. I slowly turn to see Lance fumble into the house. He runs into the living room.

"Casey," he says, out of breath.

As he comes to my side and looks through the waiting mortuary window, his face pales. He clamps a hand over his mouth.

Around Aunt Martha's wrist is a string that leads to the top of the wall, to a hook and the hanging bell. A rat scurries away from her face where he's taken more than a few huge bites out of her, leaving another open wound. She twists back and forth, the bell rings like rapid-fire and brings me back to my senses.

"Let's get her out of there," Lance cries.

I force myself to work with him. There's no other choice. I follow him through the door and the rats scatter as Martha continues to writhe back and forth.

"Hold my phone," I say to him.

He takes it and lifts it overhead where now I can see the full extent of her injuries. I stare in horror. Her lower limbs have been hacked off. Makeshift bandages are tied around two bloody stumps where dozens of rats have feasted on her exposed flesh.

"Hurry, Casey," Lance says. "She's bleeding to death."

"I can see that," I snap.

I work to unbind her wrists but the damage to her body is severe.

"Stay still," I say to her. The binding is tight, too tight. "I need scissors," I say.

Martha's eyes bulge even more at the mention of a blade.

"Call the police," I cry frantically to Lance. "I don't know what to do."

Just as he's about to dial, there's a sound just beyond the mortuary window.

Our eyes both shift to the noise.

The base of the watching chair rattles and straightens itself to a flat surface. Then, the four wooden legs of the chair that I broke off fly one at a time like weapons from where they lay scattered. One, in the corner of the interior room lifts into the air. It hits Lance in his head.

He teeters to the side, holding his skull.

Another flies through the mortuary window. I duck as the wood rips through the air.

Each leg finds its position on the base of the chair. It uprights itself and shifts back into position before the window.

A scream tunnels into my throat. I press my hands over my mouth as the same familiar sound of weight eases into the seat. "Alfred Kessler," I whisper.

"There's something watching us," Lance says, a trickle of blood leaks down his temple.

"Not us," I say. "Her." I turn to face Aunt Martha. "He wants to see if she'll live or die."

"She'll die if we don't move faster."

"Hold on," I say to Martha as I try to untie the restraints again.

"She's trying to say something," Lance says.

It pains me to see the damage. Tears flow down my cheeks.

Her eyes widen and I can see the redness and strain in the white of her eyes. She moans and I try my best to get her to stop moving so that I can reach in and get what looks like a piece of her own clothing out of her mouth.

"Stop moving," I beg as my fingers work to grab hold of it.

But her muffled scream is full of panic and desperation like she's fighting to stay alive.

"I need you to hold her head still," I say to Lance.

He goes to her opposite side and places his phone on the ledge then holds her head between his hands.

She twists back and forth.

She's screaming and fighting him, and her eyes are rolling around like she's about to lose consciousness.

"Hold on," I say as I reach into her mouth and pull out the rag.

Her scream pierces through the room. "You!" she shrieks. "Get away from me! You did this!"

"Aunt Martha," I say, trying to keep her with me, but it's too late.

She shifts her eyes from me. Her gaze goes straight through the window, back to the watching chair and then she's gone.

"W-what happened?" Lance asks.

"I-I don't know," I cry out.

"Is she still alive?"

I reach down and feel her wrist. I'm no expert but there's no sensation at all. I press my ear to her chest. No heart beat. "She's dead," I say. "She's gone," I yell at the chair. "Are you satisfied?"

The base collapses. All four legs scatter and the flat part rattles to silence.

Lance stares at the chair then back to me. "Who are you talking to?"

My chest heaves. "I don't know. I don't know what's happening." Her accusatory words have shaken me. As if I could've done this—*but how*? I rack my brain trying to remember. The words of our fight flash through my mind.

The broken door frame. *Had I done that?* Did I take the bell as another trophy? No way I could have done this. My eyes flash to Lance. He seems to have the same questions I do. The same fear of calling the police. The same worries that we will be charged. My mind begins to break apart again.

"What are we going to do?" he asks.

"We have to bury her," I say as I grab a shard of glass from the floor and begin trying to cut through the restraints. "No one can know about this."

Lance stands there. He slowly takes the phone to his heart.

"Why did you leave me this morning?" I demand.

"The detectives," he says. "I couldn't tell you."

I shake my head. Whatever secrets he's hiding, I've had enough. "You left me," I hiss.

I finally snap the restraint in two. "I don't know what's happening," I say. "Until I do, I-I can't let anyone think I did this. I fought with her. I don't remember everything about last night." My mind feels so broken again, but the demolition crew will be here soon. "They can't find us here in the house with a dead and tortured body."

Finally, the second restraint snaps. "Will you help me?"

"Bury her?" he asks. His face pales.

"You said I should tell you if I needed help. We have to move her body before the demolition crew comes in."

"W-where?" he asks.

"In the backyard." My head bobbles as I try to keep my composure. The tricks my sick mind plays on me are too much. I try to remember doing this, forcing her to the mortuary just like I did with Ally. Watching her struggle as I sat in the chair enjoying every minute of her torture. Dozens of fantasies have played out in my mind just like this. Seeing Aunt Martha suffer for all her years of nastiness would be something I wanted, but this? Did I do this?

As I work on her last restraint, there suddenly appears from the corner of the mortuary two yellow eyes. I stop what I'm doing. My body stiffens. "Something else is here," I say.

Lance follows my gaze.

"Hurry," he whispers, and I feel it in my soul. Whatever that thing is in the corner is evil. It rises from hell.

Finally, the last restraint breaks and Lance pulls Martha's limp body, or what's left of it, over his shoulder and carries her out of the mortuary. I quickly follow him, away from the yellow eyes and back out into the living room.

Blood trickles down the back of Lance's shirt and leaves a trail on the floor.

"How do we get into the backyard?" he asks, scanning the far end of the room.

"The stairs," I say. "I think they lead out back."

We walk down the hallway.

I swing open the door and feel my body freeze as the light from my phone falls on the splintered steps, and all I can think of is escaping from Phish's torture chamber in the basement of an old house that looked just like this.

"I-I can't do this," I yell and turn back, slamming the door closed.

"What's going on?" Lance's voice calls out.

"Let's just go," I say.

"We can't walk out with her body," he says. "There are people out there. They probably heard her scream."

"They're probably used to screams around here," I say. "Just put her on the couch."

"Our prints are everywhere now," he says. "The demolition crew will come in here to check for homeless people before tearing it down."

The lump in my throat feels like a scream. He's right.

There's no way I can leave Aunt Martha now a crumpled corpse without legs and a torn-up face on the floor. I imagine the demolition crew coming in to see this mess. There will be an investigation and I've already told the detectives I've been here. That, plus my prints will be the nail in my coffin.

"We go fast," I say. "Then, we don't talk about this again."

He agrees and I open the basement door again. A cold wind seems to gush over us and the eerie feeling of something lingering down there makes me tense.

Lance goes first. He steps down. The wood groans as he readjusts Martha's dead weight for the next step.

"Are you coming?" he asks.

I swallow and step down, holding up the light from the phone. My heart pounds. I need another of Dr. Bruner's pills and vow to take one just as soon as I get out of here.

With my free hand, I search for a railing along the wall but there's nothing. I flash the light over the edge of the stairs and see the cold, hard cement floor below us. With every step I feel like I'm descending into the past, into something I never wanted to see again.

Aunt Martha's dead face dangles over Lance's shoulder.

There's another loud creaking and then a louder, sharp *crack!*

I shift the light to the stairs and scream out "no!" just as I feel the sense of weightlessness.

Chapter Twenty-Two

The phone flickers.

What's left of the screen light begins to fade.

Aunt Martha whispers in my ear to get up and my eyes slowly open and are met with her hard stare. Every time the light comes to life her wrecked face is there, red, strained eyes and a bulging veiny neck.

"You, horrible girl," her haunting voice says. "Wretched, horrible girl!"

The light flickers again toward the shattered staircase.

Lance's arm.

Martha's face.

I grab my phone and try to push myself up, but a piercing pain runs up my side. I flash the light down to where it hurts. A piece of wood from the staircase juts out from my calf.

Blood drips down. My head spins as I rip off my coat and tie it around my wound then try to stand, but Martha's voice is there beside me, next to my face. "Horrible, selfish brat. I'll murder you myself."

Her hands reach out and grab hold of my neck as I scramble back.

The light from the phone flickers to black.

"Leave me alone!" I yell as I try to get it to work again.

Several voices brush past my ear. I work to get the light on again, but I can feel her there. The scent of her arthritis cream is beside me and her hot breath on my neck.

I shake my phone and smack it with my palm. Sweat drips down my cheeks. The light flashes on and I spin around toward the voices. There's nothing. I swivel back and try to find Lance. Finally, I spot him buried under the wood and not moving. I climb my way over to him and move aside the broken pieces.

"Lance," I say, reaching for his arm and shaking it. "Please, wake up."

As I pull on his arm, I see red ligature marks at the wrist and realize I'm pulling on Martha's dead arm.

Easing the wood away, one plank at I time, I finally see her face. Her stare is fixed and permanent. I swallow and move through the broken debris to find Lance, spotting his familiar black jacket. I throw planks over my shoulder and dust off his face. A nail has punctured his chest and it looks like his leg is twisted in the wrong direction.

He moans and I yell, "Lance, please, wake up! Please, I need you."

His body stirs and finally after a few moments he sits up slowly, wheezing in pain. "Wh-what happened?"

"The stairs—," I point to the wood surrounding us, "they collapsed."

"Are you okay?" he asks.

My hand goes to my leg. "I'll be fine," I say. "We need to get out of here."

With one arm I help him up and we work our way out

of the wood pile through a darkened hallway to where a sliver of light pushes through a back window.

"The backyard," I say. "It's the only way out of here now."

I wince with every step as the pain in my leg throbs until I get to the back and yank open the jammed door. Outside, is quiet. Hours have gone by since entering the waiting mortuary. There's no way of knowing how long I laid there on the ground unconscious.

"Be careful," I say to him as we walk out and nearly fall into an open grave.

All around us are holes, dug every few feet, and it flashes in my mind that this is where Alfred Kessler buried the bodies that Phish delivered to him and even though they've long since been removed, there's something still unholy that lingers here.

"What about your Aunt Martha?" Lance says. "We should try and bury her."

My eyes go to his leg. Its odd angle makes me shiver. "We'll have to come back," I say as I shift his weight against me. The pain in my leg intensifies and blood seeps down into my shoe.

Sidestepping a giant hole in front of us, we move along the back edge of the house to a wall at least six-feet high with a few boards missing on the far end.

"We can get through there," I say.

Lance's face looks whiter than a sheet, and I feel him getting weaker.

"Only a little bit further, okay?"

His eyes squeeze closed. A tear streams down his cheek and when I glance at his leg again, I know it must be broken. The pain must be unbearable.

Once through the opening in the fence, I get him down the driveway and into my car.

"I'm going to pass out," he says.

"No, Lance," but before I can shake him to stay with me, his head slides over to the car window.

There's no time to drive back to Westport. I spin the car wheel and head toward Bridgeport Hospital.

Chapter Twenty-Three

"H*elp us!*"

I rush as fast as I can into the emergency room. "My boyfriend is in the car. I think his leg is broken."

A few nurses run outside.

I want to follow, but a woman stops me. "You look like you're injured, too."

The blood from my leg has soaked through my pants and pools onto the floor, leaving red footprints with each step.

She turns to another nurse and a few seconds later I'm on a gurney and a curtain is drawn around me.

"Cut off her pants," the doctor says, but the nurse is already doing it.

My heart feels like a train coming around a bend at top speed. There's a good chance I'm going to come off the rails. I'm trying as hard as I can to not scream again. I'm going to lose consciousness, too, as they stick me with a needle and the flurry of hands and faces wave around me like something from one of my worst nightmares.

"We're going to have to sedate you," the doctor says, looking more closely at me.

His heavy, dark eyebrows and deep voice feel familiar.

The nurse with the clipboard asks my name, but the doctor responds, "Casey McClair."

It's a good thing he knows me. The medication kicks in and my words pour from my mouth like molasses. "I … was … here," is all I manage to say.

The doctor nods. "I remember you. Casey, I'm Dr. Patel. I'll be taking care of you."

"My … brother," I say. "My phone … call him … please."

"Don't worry about that right now," Dr. Patel says.

In the haze of opioids, I'm sure I'm watching myself from the waiting mortuary window. There's the girl who's in between life and death. "I'm not … dead," I say, but I can't move my wrist to ring the bell.

There's a moment when I feel like I should stop trying to move. The peace of this medication courses through my veins and removes the stress of making any decisions. What's the point of fighting? In death I can finally rest.

It's not long before they move me from the emergency room to a small, private room. I'm alone for what feels like eternity until finally a nurse in blue scrubs comes into the room. She fidgets with the machines for a few moments and takes my vitals.

"Where … is he?" I mumble to her. "Lance …"

"I don't know, honey," she says. "I just started my shift. I'll try and find out, okay?"

I have to accept it because I again feel like something is coming over me. Another haze of medication. I try and look down at my leg before I zone out, but I can't. All I can do is lie there and wait and it's the worst feeling, the loss of control that I hate the most.

THERE's no telling how long I've been sedated, but when I finally come around there's a tray of what looks like dinner food in front of me. I'm somewhere different. A second or third room. I don't know but when I look at my leg, I can see that my wound has been fixed. Along my calf there are at least twenty stitches that run vertical and small pieces of white tape, too. I slowly cover it with the bedsheet. This room is quiet. I slowly sit up and take the top off the plate and examine the cold beef, watery sauce with mushy peas, and rock-hard bread.

I'm starving, so I attempt the peas and eat two spoonfuls before pushing away the tray.

"You're eating, that's good," Doctor Patel says as he comes into the room.

"Is there anything else?" I beg.

"I'll see what I can do." He pulls back the bedsheet and examines my leg. "You lost a lot of blood. Pretty bad gash. We had to flush it because of the wood splinters and other debris, but no bone break.

"So, I'll be okay?" I ask.

"You'll be fine," he says.

As far as hospital visits go at Bridgeport this sounds like good news and there's something reassuring in the doctor's demeanor.

"How did the injury happen?" he asks, pulling a rolling chair closer.

"I was in an old house," I say. "I shouldn't have been there. The stairs collapsed."

"That explains the wood splinters," he says.

My neck feels stiff as I try to turn it.

He notices and says, "I'll get you some treatment for that."

I nod my thank you and begin to think about Kenny. "Do you have my phone?" I ask.

Dr. Patel continues to write a few things in my chart and then says, "You'll get it back when you leave. Don't worry, we keep everything safe for our patients."

I want to believe him, but that's not been my experience, and getting out of Bridgeport Hospital yet again moves to the top of my to-do list.

"Let's focus on you for right now, shall we?" he asks. He begins to shine a light in my eyes. "You overdosed two days ago?"

My throat feels dry. There's no sense in lying. They know everything. It's in the chart. "It was a mistake," I say. "I had a fight with someone, and I took too much medication."

Dr. Patel's chin juts up and I can't tell if he's listening to me or evaluating me or doing something else, so I wait until finally he says, "You mentioned coming in here with someone else."

"I did." I sit up. "His name is Lance Crux. His leg was injured."

"That name sounds familiar," Dr. Patel says.

It dawns on me that bringing Lance here may have been a mistake. I didn't even think that maybe his memories of Bridgeport Hospital are just as bad as mine are of the morgue.

"You must know him," I say. "He works here in the morgue and I think he may have been a patient here a long time ago."

"I can't speak about another patient," Dr. Patel says. "I can tell you that you came in here alone."

"But someone here must know what happened to him." I begin to describe Lance and his injuries, but the doctor still shakes his head.

"Casey, I only saw you come through the door."

"I don't mean to be rude, doctor, but this hospital is by far the worst place I've ever been. How can you not know what happened to him?"

There's a look that passes over his face as he glances down at his notes and writes something. "I think you should talk to someone."

"Who?" I demand. "Is there a hospital administrator? Someone who keeps track of patients."

"You need a psychiatrist," he says, bluntly.

"I have one," I say. "Dr. Edgar Bruner, court-ordered."

I strain my neck to see his notes, but he pulls back and says, "I will contact him for you and bring him here. I think you need to rest, Casey. I remember what happened to you over the summer. It's certainly possible with additional stress that you may have had a break with reality."

My mind races as I try to push myself up, but the doctor's right. I can't go anywhere until I get a hold of what's going on. I lean back and say, "I was getting better. At least I thought I was."

He gives me a weak smile and disappears.

A few moments later two orderlies come into the room and lift the railing on either side of the bed. They disconnect me from the machine monitoring my blood pressure and other vitals.

Before I can figure out what's happening, they're pushing my bed down a hall and into an elevator.

A woman stands in the corner clutching her purse to her chest. She gets out on the sixth floor.

Once she leaves, one of the orderlies pulls out a key and inserts it into the elevator panel. He turns it and the elevator continues its ascent. We keep going up to unnumbered floors when finally, it stops and I feel myself pushed out, buzzed through into another passage, past several patients who sit in similar beds as mine.

It smells of vomit and disinfectant.

My heart races as I try to sit up, but the second orderly holds me down.

"Steady there," he says.

They continue to push me into a room with white walls and bars on the windows. I shake my head. It's nearly dawn. I've been gone the whole night. Kenny must be so worried.

The early morning light shines through and ice forms around the edges of the window frame. The room is cold. My gown is hardly enough. I pull the blanket tight to my chin.

Once the orderlies secure the bed to the corner wall, they hook me back up to the machines and hang my IV drip.

"Now don't go and do something stupid," one of them says.

"Like what?" I ask.

The second orderly chimes in. "Plenty of the psych patients find ways to make their situation worse."

I chew on my lip as they turn and walk out of the room, locking the door behind them. I sink back into the hard pillow behind me and try not to let my worries take hold. If only I had stayed home and not gone back to the waiting mortuary. I'm not sure how long I'll stay in the room but the tense feeling of being locked in begins to creep back into my mind and I don't like it. I don't want to be here, but it somehow feels eerily familiar.

It's not long before a nurse opens the door. She's older and wears an out-of-date white nurse uniform that reminds me of something from decades ago. The name Josephine is pinned to one of her pockets. Her jet-black hair is pulled into a tight bun beneath her white cap. The red lipstick on her thin lips is smeared. She places a tray on the table in front of me and then moves around to check the IV bag and my vitals.

"I'm Nurse Joe," she says. Her voice is gruff.

"Is there any word on my brother?"

"Eat your food," she orders.

There's a strange smell in the air. As I lift the plate cover, I feel myself gag. Something that resembles leaky eggs in grayish water. I push it away.

"You need to eat if that leg's going to heal," she says.

"I can't eat this," I say. "I won't eat it."

"Your choice." She shrugs and takes the tray away.

"You must have something else. Crackers? Toast?"

She reaches into her pocket and pulls out a crumbling packet of peanut butter crackers and tosses them to me. "You won't have another meal until lunch."

"What about my brother?" I ask again. "Has he asked for me?"

Again, she doesn't answer.

"Did they say anything about the boy I came in with, Lance Crux."

She ignores me.

I slowly open the packet and stuff one of the crackers in my mouth. The taste is off. I spit it out in my hand. A tiny white worm wiggles out of the peanut butter. I scream and throw the packet against the far wall.

Nurse Joe smiles, a wicked grin broadens her face and reminds me of the way Devin Phish used to look when he got excited.

It sends shivers down my spine.

"I'll be back," she says and locks the door.

My stomach twists with hunger. All I can think about is ordering a large pizza. I fling back the blanket and take a look at my leg. The gash is red and itchy. I have to get out of here and the only way that's going to happen is if I can walk. As I swing my legs over to the side, I try putting pressure on the injured one. It stings, but I can do it and a few moments later I'm up and at the door.

I twist the handle and scream out, "Let me out of here!" I bang on the door.

After a few moments, I feel tired again and shrink back to the bed. They can't hold me without consent. At least my parents' consent. I claw at my face. The stress of being locked in is too much as I fold into myself and try not to lose what little is left of my fractured mind. If only I can keep myself sane, but I'm not even sure what that is anymore.

I slowly turn my gaze to the window. The world outside. That's what will keep me grounded. The snow has melted and the tiny icicles that formed in the night drip down leaving streaks of water on the frame. I push myself up to see down to the street. Cars pass and the steam from nearby rooftops drifts up to a dawning sky. My thoughts are of Lance. If only I could know if he was okay. In the distance, rays of sun begin to thread through the dirty streets. The shadows creep along the sidewalks and buildings, pushing forward the day and I think of Aunt Martha, lying down there in the basement of the mortuary, her dead, dismembered body, and Kenny at home, not even knowing that I left.

And, my tennis bracelet—gone again along with everything I came into the hospital with. A part of me wonders if I was always bound for this hospital's psych ward. If somehow it was written in the stars, the same ones that fade now as the sun rises, leaving me once again alone and frightened.

Chapter Twenty-Four

The door clicks open.

Dr. Bruner forces himself past Nurse Joe and into the room.

"Casey," he says, breathless. "What's happened?"

As much as the man irritates me, I'm grateful to see him if it means he can help pass a message to Kenny. I shake my head, not even sure where to begin or how to answer him.

His eyes scan down to my leg. "How was she injured?" he demands.

Nurse Joe scowls. "A fall," she says and hands him the notes.

He swipes through the information then shifts to sit on the edge of the bed. As he scans my face and takes my pulse, I begin to wonder if Dr. Bruner is my only lifeline to the outside world.

"I need to get out of here," I say.

He pats my hand. "I'll work on it."

"The doctor in the emergency room said I may have had a break with reality."

"You've had too much stress," he says. "He's right. You need to rest now. They've started you on a new type of drug, one that will help you with the hallucinations."

Hallucinations? "But, I'm better now. At least better than a few months ago."

Dr. Bruner inches closer and says, "Dr. Patel wrote in your chart that you believe there are people with you who are just not there."

I bite my lip as I remember hearing Phish's voice, then Grandmother, Ally, and Aunt Martha.

"Trauma can be hard to recover from," he says. "There's only so much a person can handle, but if you rest—"

"How can I rest when I'm starving?" I say, glaring at Nurse Joe. "I haven't eaten since yesterday."

Dr. Bruner shifts to stare her down and Nurse Joe slowly backs out of the room. "I'll go find her something to eat," she says.

"Please, Dr. Bruner," I say, pulling his attention back. "I can't stay here."

"I'll try and find a way to have you moved. Maybe there's a facility over in Westport that would be better for you."

My gaze goes to the four white walls and bars on the window. "It feels like I'm trapped again."

"You deserve better than this," he says. "I'll see to it."

His determination to help me changes my whole outlook of him. Maybe I was too quick to dismiss him. "I know I didn't take our sessions together as seriously as I should have," I say. "But I did what you told me. I wrote in the journal."

"Good," he says. "That's the first step."

I don't tell exactly what I wrote. Instead, I say, "I was angry about what happened to me. I know that now."

"Naming the emotions will help you reconnect with yourself."

"I've dealt with the past, Dr. Bruner, and I'm ready to move on."

"Writing out your feelings was just the first step," he says. "It may take months of processing what you went through."

I pick at the blanket as I say, "I thought I could speed it up. That I could heal myself faster if dealt with the past like you said."

Dr. Bruner raises a brow. "What exactly do you mean?"

"I went back," I say. "To the mortuary."

"Alone?"

"No," I say. "I went with a friend. His name is Lance. I couldn't have done it without him."

"Casey, that was very reckless. It could be the reason why your recovery has slowed."

"But it hasn't," I say with confidence. "The other day I felt something inside myself. Lance was near and for just a moment I felt I could be happy. That maybe anything was possible."

"No." He shakes his head. "What you did going back to the mortuary was reckless and could've caused you to have a complete disconnect with reality, if it hasn't already."

"I haven't lost my mind."

"The mention of Lance might be a sign that you've regressed."

I lift my hand to my head. Why won't anyone believe me that I came into this hospital with him? "Dr. Bruner you have to believe me and find out where he was taken."

"You need to focus on yourself right now, okay?"

There's a pang in my chest, but I know he's right. I can't do anything for Lance while I'm locked up here and no one seems to care about him being gone more than me.

"Let's focus on the mortuary for just a minute," he says. "What exactly happened when you went back?"

"At first, I was scared of it, but it got better. Lance helped me see that. It was just a room. A room in an old house. Nothing more. All the fears I had were starting to go away until…." My mind flashes to Aunt Martha.

"What is it?" he asks.

I lower my chin.

"What else did you see?"

"Dr. Bruner, my Aunt Martha is in that house."

He searches my eyes. There's a hint of incredulity in his stare.

"Please, you have to believe me. I'm not hallucinating this. Someone killed her." I begin to think back to her reaction when I tried to help her. The way she shouted that I did this.

"What is it, Casey?" he asks.

"I think it may have been me," I whisper, "but I don't know how."

"We've talked about this. You killed your perpetrator, Devin Phish. You did what you had to. You didn't kill anyone else."

Before I can tell him what she said, Nurse Joe pushes open the door. She comes into the room with another tray. I ignore her and go on.

"Dr. Bruner, you have to believe me. Please, go to the waiting mortuary. You'll see. Her body is in the basement of Kessler's Funeral Home.

Nurse Joe's face doesn't change as she lowers the tray in front of me.

The doctor sighs. "Casey, why do you think you killed your Aunt Martha?"

"I don't know," I mutter as Nurse Joe pulls back to the door and hovers there. "When I killed Devin Phish, I didn't feel frightened."

"How did you feel?" he asks.

"Satisfied," I say.

"It must be hard to admit that," he says.

I rub my brow. "I laughed when I did it. He would never hurt me or anyone else ever again. I had taken a life, but I had also taken a threat out of the world. That feeling never left me. In my blackouts, I felt that need for revenge."

Dr. Bruner slowly stands. His eyes turn serious. "Perhaps you are capable of something more."

"Will you still help me?" I beg.

"My job is to always help my patient. I will do what I think is best for you."

It feels as if the chance of getting out of this room any time soon vanishes.

"Why don't you try eating something?" he says.

I glance down to the tray and take the lid off the plate. In front of me is a steaming pile of pasta. I inhale the scent. My mouth waters.

"Go on," Dr. Bruner says. "Eat something. Try to relax."

He turns to Nurse Joe who still stands at the door and says something about the dose of my medication and that he'd like to talk to her in private outside.

I take a look in the drink, something orange. Holding it up, I examine the contents to make sure there's nothing strange floating inside of it and then take a sip.

Nurse Joe watches me from just outside the room and when Dr. Bruner is done talking, she smiles somehow enjoying the maliciousness of me not knowing what I'm drinking.

As I raise a bite of pasta to my mouth, Dr. Bruner turns back and says, "Casey, I think in the next few days, you're going to have more clarity. I'll come back and see you. We can discuss more next time."

"But, no!" I let my fork clatter to the plate. "You can't go yet. Someone has to help my stepbrother. He's home by himself. He'll be worried about me. I didn't even have time to tell him I was leaving or where I was going."

"I'll check on him," Dr. Bruner says.

"My parents will come home now," I say. "They'll have to now."

"Just rest, Casey." Dr. Bruner turns to leave. "It's clear you are still unwell. Even if you have made progress, you still need to rest. You will feel better soon."

Once he's gone, I feel there's some hope. Dr. Bruner will return. I won't be another forgotten psych patient. I take another sip of my juice and eat the rest of my pasta, finally feeling the pang of hunger dissolve.

More time passes and I can't stand the sight of the walls and the way the lock clicks every time Nurse Joe enters and leaves. I'm a prisoner again, but I have to do what Dr. Bruner said. It's the only way I'm going to get better. I sleep for an hour or two until the lock clicks again and Nurse Joe reenters. Time feels irrelevant now. It's only about her checks of my vitals and recheck of my stitches.

"Are you this attentive to all the patients on the psych ward?" I ask her while she dabs ointment on my wound.

"I try to show equal care to each patient." She pinches my leg as I squirm to get away from her and once again that strange smile broadens her face.

"You like torturing your patients, don't you?"

"That's enough of that," she says. "I've been on this ward for decades now. Never a complaint."

"I guess the people you kill can't really complain, can they?"

Her eyes flash dark as she leans in. "Don't forget who gives you your medications."

· It's a threat. As real as they come, and I believe her.

When she steps back, she smooths out her uniform. "Now, enough of that silly talk. You've been through a lot. First that horrible kidnapper and now your own torment."

"What do you know about me?" I ask.

"Everyone on both sides of the river knows about what you went through." She leans in and whispers, "I'm glad you killed him, though. Devin Phish was a real bastard."

"Would you be glad if I told you he's not the only one I've killed?"

She smiles, again with that strange half-cocked grin. "That's just your sickness talking. Pretty soon everything's going to settle down again." She puts a little something into my IV bag.

"Was is that?" I demand, ready to tear out my needle.

"The same thing you've been taking since you got here, dear. No worries. Just relax. You'll feel much better in no time."

She turns and leaves the room. Only this time there's no click of the lock.

There's a slow, steady hum like static. I can feel a strangeness in my body as the medication seeps into my veins. The tightness in my legs and chest evaporates. There's a freedom in me that I haven't felt in weeks and I can't help but wonder what she put in my IV. Whatever it is, I feel upbeat and strong.

I slowly go to the door and pull the handle. It easily opens. Pulling the IV out is not the worst thing I've ever done. I've taken a breathing tube from my throat and fought off a serial killer with broken ribs. Once the needle is out, I cover the bleed with some of the bandage from my leg and creep back to the door.

Outside in the hallway, there's another nurse working to calm her patient and no Nurse Joe in sight.

I sneak down the hall as fast as the pain in my leg will let me, past several rooms, and toward what looks like a barrier between the ward and the outside world up ahead. As I rush closer, a man, stark naked, and with vacant eyes, steps in front of me. I nearly scream as I bring my fist to my mouth.

A voice calls out from his bedroom and I quickly find what looks like it might be a storage closet and slip inside, watching through the crack in the door as two orderlies drag him back into his room.

The sweat on my brow drips down my cheek. My pulse beats like rapid fire. I quickly wipe my face. Again, I peer out the door. The hallway is clear as I step out and make my way to the exit. As I pass the other rooms of the psych ward, I see one patient after another lying in their beds. Tormented eyes watch me as I slip past. In one of the rooms a man turns his head and I feel my lunch push up.

"Who's there?" he calls out. Half his head is missing. His brain lies exposed with several machines attached to wires.

My hand flies to my mouth to cover what feels like a scream beginning to surface. I push off the wall and rush to the exit. Just as I'm about to reach out a hand, I see Detective Sanchez standing there on the other side of the glass-paneled window.

Chapter Twenty-Five

"*Casey McClair!*"

Nurse Joe shuffles closer. When she sees the detective coming through the door she calmly says, "That's okay, dear. Your room is back this way." She grabs hold of my arms and turns me around as Detective Sanchez follows us.

"What's going on?" the detective asks.

"She's just had a stronger dose of her medication," Nurse Joe says. "It gives them a little boost in confidence."

"She was trying to get out," Detective Sanchez says as we reenter the room.

"No, no." Nurse Joe gets me back into my bed and tucks the sheets in tight. "We wouldn't want our patients roaming the streets of Bridgeport, would we?"

I swallow and my eyes flit from her to the detective and back again. A part of me doesn't want to hear why Detective Sanchez is here or what she's going to say. Detectives never come with good news, do they? If she says it's about Kenny, I know I'll be sick. If she's come to arrest me, I'll go without a fight.

"Can you give us a few minutes?" Detective Sanchez asks Nurse Joe.

"Of course, but not too long. I'll need to reinsert that IV. I'll leave the door open, but no adventures again." She wags a finger at me and leaves.

For some reason I feel like Nurse Joe wanted me to escape, and I can't help to think if it's because people like her want the chaos. Maybe she wants to see what someone in my condition will do out there on the streets or what will be done to me. Before I can figure it out, though, Detective Sanchez steps closer breaking into my thoughts.

"How's it going, Casey?" she asks.

"I'm in the psych ward," I say, "so not very good."

She presses her lips together.

"Whatever it is just say it," I demand.

"We found Ally Parker's finger."

I cringe. "Where?"

"Your car, Casey. Glove compartment."

My shoulders drop as I remember stashing it there, and accept I'm screwed. Whether I'm in the psych ward or the state penitentiary my days of freedom are over.

"Do you want to tell me how it got there?"

I can only tell her what I know. "I put it there," I say.

She folds her arms across her chest. "Do you want to revise the statement you gave me the other day?"

"No," I say. "Everything I told you was true."

"Your version of the truth," she says.

"Who else's?"

"Okay, let's go over this again. You followed her to the park."

"Every day," I say.

"You wanted her dead?"

"Yes," I admit. "Ally Parker deserved to die. She was

selfish and stuck-up. Devin Phish should've taken her, not me."

"So, you killed her? Because you were mad that he kidnapped you and not Ally."

I don't know how to answer that. "I can't say for sure that I did."

"You had her finger in a jewelry box," Detective Sanchez says.

"The finger ended up in my bag," I say. "I don't know how. I took it out and put it in the jewelry box."

"Why?"

"I needed to put it somewhere."

"You know how this looks, right?" She cocks her head. "Are you trying to tell me that you stalked this girl, wished her dead, concealed evidence, but you didn't do it?"

"That's what I'm telling you because I don't know!" I hate that I raised my voice. It will only make Nurse Joe come back in, but I can only admit to what I'm sure of.

"Anything else?" she asks, dumbfounded.

"Yes," I say. "My Aunt Martha is dead, too. Her body is in the basement at Kessler's Funeral Home."

She takes a step back and scoffs. "You really did it this time."

I want to argue with her but a part of me thinks she's probably right.

"Just go check the waiting mortuary," I whisper.

"Where you went back to," she says. "With your boyfriend, Lance."

I lift my head. "Yes," I say. "It's how I ended up here."

"Why don't you tell me how you ended up finding your Aunt Martha in the waiting mortuary?"

"There was a picture of her left in my house. I saw her strapped to one of the tables. I had to go. I thought she left us, had enough of Kenny and I, but when I went to the house, I found her, tortured. She was on one of the tables just like in the picture. Detective Sanchez, I tried to help her. Her legs were gone. A rat had been chewing on her face. If it wasn't for Lance, I wouldn't have had the courage to try to free her, but when I did, she died."

Detective Sanchez has the same look on her face that Dr. Bruner gave me.

"What's the harm in checking it out?" I ask.

She shakes her head. "That house is scheduled for demolition," she says, pulling out her phone and texting something. "Damn, there's no reception here."

"If you go there," I say, "you'll see."

She sighs and takes a step closer. "Casey, I don't know what's happened since you got away from Devin Phish, but I know what evil looks like and I don't think you're that. What I'm looking at right now is a very sick young woman."

"Will you go to the mortuary?" I ask. "See if I'm telling the truth."

"I will," she says, taking a step back and disappearing out into the hallway.

Chapter Twenty-Six

T*ime feels different here.*

I sleep with only a few passing dreams. One of my mother. She sips a Mai Tai near a sparking, blue ocean. The sand is warm and soft like cookie dough. I pad my way to her side. She throws back her head and laughs at the sight of me trying to avoid the sharp rocks on my way, but I make it there and fall into her arms.

She smooths back my hair and says she misses me and soon everything will be better. I already know she's right, and when I wake, I feel lighter than I've felt ever in my life. The jagged edges of weeks of bad dreams feel like they're lifting, and at my core, whatever lurked there, dark and heavy, feels as if it might be fading.

I lie in the darkness of the room and for some reason I don't feel afraid or trapped.

A few moments later, the door opens. Nurse Joe is there with Dr. Bruner.

"It's time to go," she says, handing me a plastic bag. "Dr. Bruner is here to take you to a different facility."

I take the bag and turn to look outside. It's the dead of

the night, but who am I to object? I let her take the IV from my arm, carefully this time and with a proper bandage, then they both step from the room while I change back into my familiar clothes and snap my bracelet back around my wrist. I take out my phone and turn it on. Once it lights up, I search for texts but there are none, so I tuck it into my back pocket, and finish pulling my hair back into a ponytail.

"Ready?" Nurse Joe asks as she brings in a wheelchair.

I slowly nod, sit down, and let her push me from the room into the empty hallway.

Dr. Bruner looks tired and I can only imagine the strings he had to pull to get me transferred.

"Thank you," I say to him as Nurse Joe pushes me toward the exit.

He smiles and squeezes my hand.

Nurse Joe buzzes us out, she waves goodbye with the same sick grin on her face.

I won't miss her.

A few minutes later Dr. Bruner wheels me past the front desk where a sleepy looking security guard leans back in his chair and then out the sliding doors into the cold night.

"My car is around the side," he says.

I take a deep breath. The frozen air burns in my lungs, but I'm grateful for it. As I twist back to look at Bridgeport Hospital, I know I'll never return. I wasn't there for very long, but somehow time has slipped away from me and it feels like there's space between me and the real world, like I can handle moving back into it and whatever comes my way.

"My brother," I ask Dr. Bruner. "Is he okay?"

"He's fine," Dr. Bruner says. "I checked on him a few hours ago. He's holding up well but misses you."

"I've really made a mess of things with him, haven't I?"

"From my brief conversation with him, I believe Kenny is much stronger than you know."

It's a relief to hear Dr. Bruner say that when all I can think of is how badly he needs me to be the pillar of strength. I quickly pull out my phone and raise it, hoping it will bring back my reception. After a moment or two it connects and I begin to text Lance, but Dr. Bruner glances over and frowns.

"Not now, Casey," he says. "Let's give that a rest."

"Just one text," I say. "I need for him to know I'm okay."

Dr. Bruner pulls out his car keys, unlocks the doors of his four-door sedan, and helps me from the wheelchair into the passenger seat.

"Buckle up," he says.

I do quickly while he returns the wheelchair to the curb and then rushes to get into the driver's seat.

"Thank you for getting me out of there," I say once the car starts moving.

"You're not totally in the clear yet," he says. "I'll still need to check you in at another facility."

"Where?"

"It's a small clinic," he says. "It's the best place for your final stages of recovery."

"You think I'm recovering, too?" I ask, suddenly uplifted.

"There comes a point, Casey, when medications no longer work. The brain begins to create what's called a new normal. I believe you're entering into that phase."

A new normal. I think to myself what that might look like. Gone are the days of fear and anger. I imagine a new life and for the first time it feels within grasp. Not just something that I hope for, but something I can feel and touch.

As Dr. Bruner winds his car around the backroads of the hospital and into the neighborhoods of Bridgeport, I begin to look around and recognize the familiar streets and homes. I chew on my lip, thinking about if Detective Sanchez discovered Aunt Martha's body in the basement.

"Dr. Bruner, can we make one more stop?"

"Casey, it's late."

"Please," I say. "I know you didn't believe me before when I told you about Aunt Martha being dead in the funeral home, but it was real. I sent Detective Sanchez there to look into it."

"Then you should let the detectives do their job."

"But Dr. Bruner if I know whether or not they found Aunt Martha's body there, I'll be able to go into the new clinic knowing if I've really lost touch with reality or not. Please I need to know."

He glances to me and then turns the wheel away from the main road that leads to the Bridgeport Bridge and back toward Kessler's Funeral Home. "Against my better judgment," he says.

Glancing out the window, I know what he means, but if I played everything by the book and waited for Detective Sanchez's call or visit, I know I'd slowly wear myself out with overthinking. As we near the street, I vow that if there's no trace of Aunt Martha's body and torture then I'll fully commit to the clinic's therapeutic techniques; no matter what they are, I'll accept just how sick I am.

As Dr. Bruner pulls in front of the house, I notice three more homes on the block are gone and the bulldozers have moved closer. It's still night and there are none of the construction sounds from when I was here last, but the emptiness of the neighborhood makes Kessler's Funeral

Home look lonelier than ever. I can't help but notice there's no yellow tape fluttering in the wind. No sign of Detective Sanchez's car. No police activity, either.

He helps me out of the car.

There's a sting in my leg, but I can walk on it and together we head up the path to the front window.

"You have to climb over," I say to Dr. Bruner who's standing to my side.

"There's broken glass," he says. "This doesn't look safe."

My chest heaves. "It's not," I say, "but I still have to go in and look." Before he can stop me, I climb over the ledge, raising my injured leg with both hands and lowering it to the other side, then the other, and take a moment to make sure I can bear the weight without crying out in pain. It's a slow process but with deep breaths and grit I manage to finally stand and flick on my phone's flashlight.

A moment later, Dr. Bruner climbs over. His shoes crunch down on the glass.

"Be careful," I say. "There are rats everywhere and by the sound of things, I think they get worse at night." Their scratching claws travel up and down the walls as Dr. Bruner watches me.

I twist my light to the hallway next to the kitchen. "We have to go over there," I say.

The door to the fallen staircase is still open. I brace myself.

Dr. Bruner follows and together we make our way toward it.

The floorboards creak with each step. I hold my breath that they won't break apart again and send us tumbling down to the basement. As I reach the door, I hold up my light and shine it down to what had been the staircase. Now, it's a giant empty abyss of scattered and jagged piles of wood. I turn the light left then right as I search for Martha's body.

"I know she's down here," I say as the light finally falls on a face. "There," I say, shining the light on her. Only as I lean closer, it becomes clear I'm not looking at Aunt Martha.

Chapter Twenty-Seven

"*Detective Sanchez?*"

She slowly opens her eyes. She's tied tight to a chair beside the fallen staircase.

"Casey?" she says, squinting. "Casey! Get out of there!"

Before I can do anything, Dr. Bruner pulls me away from the door.

My eyes go wide as his face suddenly turns hard.

"Have you seen enough?" He slams the basement door shut. The house shudders.

"What's going on?" I demand. The light from my phone shines into his eyes.

"This is your final therapeutic session," he says. "The perfect clinic with all the tools needed to solidify your new normal."

My pulse races as I swing my fist at his head, but he grabs hold of it and slowly twists my hand as I scream out, "stop!"

"You shouldn't fight the treatment. After tonight, you'll finally be cured."

He snatches my phone and smashes it beneath his heel so that only blackness surrounds us.

Powerless, I feel his hands grab my shoulders. He marches me away from the hall. Panic descends into my body as I writhe to get away from him.

Despite the pitch black, I feel a sudden blow to my injured leg and know he's just kicked my wound. I wince in pain and scream out.

"It would be better if you did what I told you," he hisses into my ear.

I can feel his hot breath behind me, and the artificial scent of his cheap cologne mixed with adrenaline.

"Are you going to kill me?" I ask, still hobbling in pain in the dark.

He doesn't answer. Instead, he shoves me from behind and I fall onto the dirty, rat-infested couch.

I gasp as something squirms beneath me. I inhale a cloud of dust and gag. As I fight to figure out where the doctor is, my mind unravels. In the dark there are whispers. I press my fists to my temples. I won't go back to that. I won't be imprisoned or tormented another day.

Dr. Bruner hovers nearby. His breath is the only sound now as if he's frightened away the rodents and steadied the house in anticipation.

Pulling myself to the edge of the couch, I wait for what might come. A fist in the dark. Another kick to my wound. Maybe something worse. The unknowing turns my stomach.

Finally, I feel him ease to my right side. "Ever since you escaped Devin Phish, I've been fascinated by you."

I swallow and grip the couch's frame. If only there was a moon out tonight, I could see his face, but the window beyond the living room is dark.

Then, there's the sound of a striking match and Dr.

Bruner's wicked and shadowy face appears before me. His perfectly shaved beard accentuates a snarled lip, a sinister expression I've never seen in him before.

"What do you want with me?" I demand.

"You were so strong to defeat him. A man twice your size and you fought him and won."

"I'll do the same to you," I hiss. "If you don't let me and Detective Sanchez go, I'll find a way to kill you, too."

His eyes gleam as he touches the burning match to a candle and the room begins to lighten. "It's not your physical strength I've tested. It's your mental strength."

"My mental strength?"

"Not everyone can withstand a challenge, especially on the medication I gave you."

My mind flashes to the pills. Months of anti-anxiety medication. A pill twice a day that I doubled up.

As if he's following my train of thought, he laughs and says, "Experimental medications."

"I trusted you," I say. There's a storm brewing inside of me. All of the night terrors, the torment I put Kenny and myself through. "I nearly died."

"But you didn't," he says. "You came close to death so many times. You've always survived when others would've crumbled long ago."

"Why would you do that to me?"

"You can't get better until you rid yourself of the past, of everything that was the old Casey McClair, and rebuild your new identity."

"You were trying to destroy me? You're just as sick as Phish."

He laughs and steps back. Hallucinogens have been used throughout time to process psychic wounds. You're nearly through the worst and once we've finished the last step you will be truly healed. No one will be able to hurt you ever again."

"I should've trusted my instincts about you," I say. "I thought you were a joke, but you're not. You're evil. Just as evil as Phish." A part of me wonders if he's not worse. Maniacal. Fighting a physical body is one thing, but he set me up to fight myself. My own mind was under attack.

"Did you kill Ally Parker?" I ask, point blank.

"She had to die," he says. "Her death was the first step in creating your spiral back into the trauma."

"And, her finger," I ask, "How did it get into my bag?"

"I followed you here after your all-night bender. At first, I just wanted to see your expression when you found out Ally had been kidnapped. I had planned to make an unexpected house call, but when I saw you racing out the front door of your house, I followed you. You didn't lock your car, Casey. In this neighborhood? With the crime rates soaring, I'd thought you'd make it much harder, but it was easy. I simply opened your car door and placed Ally's finger inside your bag."

"And Martha? Why did you kill her?"

"She was interfering with the process," he says. "She called me and said you were losing it. I came to the house. She said you locked yourself in your room and wouldn't come out. I broke down the door to find you near death."

"But you didn't save me," I say. "You're a doctor and you didn't do anything to help me."

"I thought you had failed," he says. "Perhaps you were not as strong as I had hoped. Your Aunt Martha was hysterical. I had to shut her up. I knocked her out then pulled my car into the garage and shoved her in the trunk."

"You tortured her," I say. "Why?"

"I had only wanted to experiment," he says. "She

screamed while I hacked off her legs. She was a fighter, too. I thought she might be able to withstand the pain, but, no, she was weak, and when I saw there was no hope, I left her to the rats."

My stomach turns as I ask, "Where is her body?"

"Buried," he says. "Out back. So many open graves to choose from. One for Detective Sanchez, too, if she fails our next experiment."

"What do you mean by *our* next experiment?" I ask.

"You can be one of the greats," he says. "You have the physical and mental strength of a true taker of life."

"A murderer," I hiss. "You want me to be like … you."

"Even better," he says. "Imagine what we could accomplish together."

While he goes on with his vision, I begin to think of the bell in the guest bathroom and the front door that was open when I woke up. A chill works its way down my spine as I consider how awful Dr. Bruner is, how he weaseled his way into becoming my court-appointed therapist, a true sociopath who can't stop his sick path of murder.

"I won't let you torture me like you did Ally and Aunt Martha."

"Of course not," he says.

"What do you want from me then? Do you expect me to fight you?"

"No," he says. "I expect you to join me."

A part of me wants to run while I have the chance. I glance back at the window. Even with my hurt leg, I think I can make it there, but leaving Detective Sanchez behind would only seal her death.

"You're much sicker than you know, Casey," he says. "I read your case file every night. A child of neglectful parents and emotional abuse. You were set up to fail."

"I haven't failed yet," I say.

"It must have been agony to watch your parents die."

My shoulders stiffen.

"On an icy road, when you were twelve. Your poor stepfather, Phil, at the wheel, lost control, swerved, and the car flipped."

His words begin to conjure a vague memory. My eyes shift back and forth as I remember Mother and Phil had just returned from being away. Kenny was at school and they'd come to pick me up first.

"The traumatic mind is interesting," Dr. Bruner says. "You've held onto the belief that your parents were merely on vacation for years now, but they're dead, Casey. They died in a tragic car accident when you were twelve."

"No," I say, slowly standing. "You're wrong."

"Come on now. It was in your case file. I know it must have been terrifying to see your mother die right there in front of you."

I reach down and touch my tennis bracelet. Slowly, the memory begins to surface. There was ice on the road, and I begin to remember the car sliding and Phil instead of turning into the slide, turned the wheel away. The car flipped twice into a snowy ice bank along the side of the road."

"Ah, you're remembering now," he says. "Yes, the tragedy was first that your mother neglected you, but you loved her dearly, didn't you?"

My eyes fill with tears. I swivel the bracelet back into place, remembering how she gave it to me. It meant so much to me. I did love her. Her death was unbearable.

I slowly step to the hallway and gaze into the hanging faded mirror on the wall as Dr. Bruner continues.

"You were alone for a long time after their deaths and sent to live with your grandmother. When she died, your stepfather's sister agreed to take you in—Aunt Martha."

Shadows from the flicker of the candle form on my face. "She blamed me for everything," I whisper. "She didn't really want me there either. She hated me for getting kidnapped, for bringing problems into her life—"

"For killing her brother," Dr. Bruner says.

"But, I didn't. It was an accident." I squeeze my eyes closed, remembering how Phil died instantly. She blamed me anyway. Not at first, but later when she agreed to take me in. It was somehow her way of punishing me. Of getting all her anger out. She put everything on me. Her words echo in my head. *You did this!* In a way, she was right. If not for me, there would be no Dr. Bruner. She wouldn't have been tortured and now lie dead in the backyard.

As I open my eyes, I feel the pain slide into me. It hurts to know the truth. I feel my shoulders tense as Dr. Bruner eases his way behind me.

Even though his presence makes me cringe, I'm too overwhelmed by the memories to fight him. The pieces inside me feel as if they're shifting.

Dr. Bruner looks over my shoulder as I gaze at my reflection. "We all deal with trauma in different ways, don't we?" he says. "Some hide from the pain. Others slip into make believe worlds. You found a friend, someone to watch over you."

My bangs cover my eye and a hint of a scar from the accident runs across my cheek. I touch it and remember. The car skidded on the ice. Phil's neck snapped. I tried to help Mother, but she was bleeding too badly. The back window had smashed open and I climbed out of the car desperate to wave down a passing car. There was nothing I could do. As I crawled to Mother's side, she took her last breaths and squeezed my hand. It was as if Lance popped up out of nowhere.

"Your Aunt Martha sent you to Bridgeport Hospital's

psych ward when you were twelve," Dr. Bruner goes on. "You spent months there until you finally got better."

"But the kidnapping triggered it again," I say, feeling hollow. "Lance isn't real."

"No," he says. "You can let him go. You're closer now, Casey. Closer than you've ever been to creating a new life for yourself."

As if spellbound, I step away from the mirror and follow Dr. Bruner back to the mortuary window where he slowly pulls back the dusty curtain.

Candles illuminate the interior room.

I ease to the window and look inside.

Two bodies lie on the metal tables. I cringe when I see Kenny's fragile and shirtless form on the first one. He's unconscious. I raise a shaky hand to my chest. My best friend, my brother. A two-inch gash to his chest leaks drops of blood to the table where Dr. Bruner must have stabbed him.

I shift my gaze to the second table where Lance fights the restraints. His eyes are open, and a rag stuffed in his mouth and even though I know he must be a figment of my imagination he looks so real and it still makes my chest ache to watch him struggle.

"Is it up to the waiting mortuary to decide if they live or die?" I ask.

"No," Dr. Bruner says. "It's up to you."

Chapter Twenty-Eight

"L*et me take Kenny out of there.*" I beg Dr. Bruner. "He's hurt. I need to help him."

"You need to finish it," he says.

I search the doctor's eyes. "Why?"

"It's the last step."

"You want me to be a murderer. Kill the one person who I know cares for me, my last tie to—"

"Your old self," he says, nudging me forward. "Kill the boy."

"And, then what? Who will I be then? What will I have?"

"The power," Dr. Bruner says. "All the power. Just like Devin Phish had, only better. You'll be stronger."

"The perfect killing machine," I whisper as I slowly make my way around the corner and into the room.

From just outside, Dr. Bruner presses his hands into the window's frame. "No one will ever hurt you again," he says.

My eyes fall on Lance. He's stopped struggling against

the restraints. His eyes, crystal blue, stare back at me and reflect my whole world.

There's no point in fighting Dr. Bruner.

The soft glow from the candles play shadows across Kenny's face. I lean over and kiss his cheek then reach up and take the string from the bell and tie it carefully around his wrist.

As I do that, he begins to stir. His eyes flutter open.

"Casey?" he asks, trying to sit up. He begins to realize where he is and struggles as I pat his shoulder.

"It's always been my job to protect you," I say.

"What am I doing here?" he demands. He struggles again, wincing in pain, and then his gaze falls on Dr. Bruner. "He brought me here, didn't he? He came to the house and told me what happened to you, about your accident. He said he'd take me to the hospital to see you, and somehow I ended up here." He twists again and sees the wound to his side.

"You need to lie still," I say. "This will only take a second."

"You bastard!" he shouts to Dr. Bruner then falls back again.

I keep a steady tone as I say, "Kenny, you're not going to like what happens next." My eyes fill with tears. "I did everything I could to make sure this never happened again. I'm sorry."

He shakes his head as I step from the room and collect one of the four wooden chair legs.

"Ah," Dr. Bruner smiles. "Crushing his skull. A good choice."

I swallow as I raise the wood above my head.

Kenny moans. "Casey," he gasps. "No."

Just then, the base of the watching chair rattles.

Dr. Bruner turns to look at it, wide-eyed, as it rises and

shifts into position outside the mortuary window. He quickly steps back. "What's this?" he asks. "A paranormal phenomenon?"

"Ghosts," I say, lowering the chair leg. "Alfred Kessler's ghost."

The doctor lays a hand on the flat surface. "Extraordinary," he says.

"He comes to watch once you've tied the string."

As Dr. Bruner eases closer, each of the watching chairs legs fly from their spots on the ground, whisking around the air nearly hitting the doctor as they finally find their spot beneath the seat.

"Amazing!" he says.

With all my might, I hold onto the last chair leg, feeling it strengthen in my hands.

"I'm sorry," I say as Dr. Bruner looks to me. "I'm not a murderer, you see. It's the waiting mortuary that decides who lives or dies."

His jaw unhinges as I let go of the chair leg. It flies fast through the mortuary window straight into Dr. Bruner's eye socket. The doctor falls back onto the base of the chair. His face oozes blood down his right cheek. His mouth remains open in an eternal scream as his body twitches. A moment later, he's thrown violently from the chair to the ground and Alfred Kessler takes his place.

"Hello, Alfred," I say. "I know how this works now. No one else watches. Only you."

I turn to Kenny. His face is pale. I work quickly to untie the string from his wrist and help him to sit up.

"This one lives," I say to Alfred and the watching chair collapses to the ground. The candles flicker and just as quickly as he arrived, the ghost of Alfred is gone.

"Do you think you can walk?" I say to Kenny.

He nods and I help him away from the table. His

wound is only surface, not deeper than the flesh. I blow out a quick breath, grateful for that, and walk him out to the front porch. "Stay here," I say, taking off my coat and wrapping it around his shoulders.

I move fast around to the side of the house and through the gate to the basement.

"Detective Sanchez," I say as I shove open the back door and rush to her side.

"Help me with the ropes," she says.

My fingers feel frozen, but I work as fast as I can to unknot them.

"I heard everything," she says.

"He wanted me to kill my brother."

Her eyes search mine. "I was wrong about you, Casey. You're a brave girl. Much braver than I could see in the hospital."

The ropes finally come free and I help her up. "Your car," I say. "It's not out front."

"He must have moved it. I'll go for help. You and Kenny stay here."

As she rushes out the basement door, I follow only to see the darkened mound in the backyard where one of the holes has been filled in.

"Detective Sanchez," I call out. My throat tightens as I go to it.

She returns to my side.

"My Aunt Martha is here," I say. "She wasn't always kind to me, but she didn't deserve this."

"Casey, no matter what Edgar Bruner said to you, you didn't do this. He did this."

I know she's right and for the first time I begin to realize I'm not the cold-blooded murder I thought. I'm a warrior. I'm a survivor.

"Go take care of your brother," she says. "There's nothing more you can do to help her."

I nod and Detective Sanchez rushes away, slipping through the fence. I follow more slowly, returning to the porch to sit beside Kenny.

"Is Aunt Martha dead?" he asks.

I nod. "He killed her," I whisper.

Kenny's eyes fill with tears. "He almost killed me, too. I would've died if not for you."

"We're going to be okay," I say.

He nods and I take a deep breath, returning my gaze to the inside of the house.

"There's just one more thing I need to do."

Chapter Twenty-Nine

Lance lies on the table.

A dim candle shines on the ledge. My feet feel frozen as I look at him. His face is still and pale. His eyes look at me longingly. The wound to his leg is worse than before. His femur juts out at a strange angle that oozes with infection.

I go to his side, reach up, and take the long string of the bell and tie it around his wrist.

The feeling of loneliness again takes hold and sinks deep into me as I begin to realize what I have to do. My head drops to my hands as I rock forward and feel the hot tears sting my face. I don't want to let him go.

The last thing in the world I want to do is live without Lance. Facing whatever comes my way without him makes me shudder, but how else can I go on when I know that keeping him would mean my most certain return to the psych ward.

A part of me just wants to leave and pretend none of this happened, wake up tomorrow with his mysterious face looming close, the feel of his warm breath at my cheek, and his promise to always be there when I need help, but as I gaze into the light of the candle, I begin to realize that I can't really be healed if I don't let him go.

I take a deep breath. The cold air of the mortuary makes expanding my lungs hard, but I continue to draw in breath after breath until there's something new surfacing inside of me. All the years of stuffing down my feelings. This is what Dr. Bruner had right. I had to come back here to deal with my feelings. To not escape from them.

I press my hand to Lance's cheek, knowing that I'm going to have to be the one to bury him. I'm going to have to mourn him. I'll have to be sad again and I don't want to. My throat tightens as I gaze at his face.

"Take the bell down," he says. "Don't let it go on. You know I won't die like the others."

I nod and pull the bell from its hook then slowly untie the string from his wrist and help him to sit up.

Lance's smile is bright. "I knew you were a fighter," he says.

I trace his scar and then feel my own across my cheek.

"You're healed now," he whispers.

I weave my fingers into his. "You're the best part of me."

"Then no more lies," he whispers.

And, it's more than I ever thought it could be. It's not two broken pieces, but one whole person. In that moment I know I can live and be everything I want. I don't have to hide or pretend. I don't have to imagine worse case scenarios or conjure guilt tripping entities. I've got everything.

I lean in and kiss Lance goodbye. His lips still feel warm as they brush against mine but then they're gone.

He's gone. The metal table is nothing more than that—a table.

I raise my fingers to my lips and whisper, "goodbye" then go out to sit with Kenny until the flashing lights of police cars and ambulances once again illuminate the night's sky.

Chapter Thirty

Toss, swing, hit.

My tennis bracelet is fixed around my wrist and with every swing of my racket it slides up my forearm and then back down, glistening beneath the lights of the indoor tennis courts. Mom would be so proud of me if she saw me now.

"You cheated on that one!" Kenny says, retrieving the ball.

"No way," I say, laughing. My skin feels alive, and I love the way this new skirt fits showing off my toned legs.

An entire month of healing from the collapsed staircase, followed by another month of training with Kenny has led me to the point of no return. I'm a force to be reckoned with as he serves another ball that bounces over the net toward me.

Thwack!

Kenny doesn't even try to return service. He watches as the ball I just hit flies into the corner well within bounds and throws his hands up. "How was I supposed to hit that?"

My hands go to my hips. "Be faster," I say.

"Do you think we can stop now?" he asks. "It's been an hour."

"Oh, fine." But, it's not really fine because I feel like I'm just getting started. Another hour of practice would give me the confidence to destroy my opponent at Saturday's match. Once the balls are all collected, we step off the court to three other people patiently waiting.

"All yours," I say to the girl. She looks familiar and I suddenly realize it's one of Ally's friends.

"You looked fierce out there, Casey," she says, and I smile my thanks and work toward the bench.

"Please tell me you have a gallon of water in that bag," Kenny says as I dig through it and hand him an electrolyte drink.

He cracks the top and downs it.

"I also have coffee," I say, pulling out a nice sized, plaid thermos. I hand him a plastic cup and unscrew the lid.

"I was hoping for a donut."

"Maybe later," I say. "After the tournament."

"You're the one competing, not me."

"Okay," I sigh as I fill the cup. "On the way home."

He takes a sip as I dig out another cup for myself and begin to think about the upcoming tournament.

"Do you think I'll be ready for the match?" I ask him. "It's been so long."

"Of course, you will," Kenny snaps back. "You've got an amazing swing and obviously you've got your strength back."

"I do, don't I?" I can't help but feel the confidence surge through my veins. Somehow going through what I did made me stronger. It should've destroyed me, but it didn't. Once my body cleared all of Dr. Bruner's experimental medication, the night terrors disappeared. As I sip my coffee, I can't help but shake the memory of those two yellow eyes in the mortuary. I remember how the mysterious dark figure stood there watching me and shiver just thinking about it, then remember the house will soon be destroyed and with it whatever lurks inside.

I glance to Kenny. A part of me can't get over how well he's doing. Despite everything that's happened, he still has hope. A part of me wants to always protect that for him. Another part of me knows he can do it for himself. That it's always been in him to be hopeful. It's not something I need to worry about anymore.

"You know," I say, "I'm thinking about the night school program."

"You should go," he says. "We'd graduate at the same time."

I imagine us both wearing caps and gowns as we cross the stage. It feels within reach especially without the worry of having to be separated from one another. I recall how the social worker said I'm old enough to take care of Kenny. As long as I worked during the day while he was in school, they'd grant me custody. It's a sense of responsibility that I know I can finally manage.

As I take a drink of my coffee, I think about my mother and how proud she'd be of me for what I've managed to overcome. But, it's not her approval I seek anymore. It's my own. Surviving two killers just proves that I can face anything, and that life must be about hope and never about fear.

"Excuse me," a voice says from behind where we sit.

I turn to see a guy, tennis racket in hand. I can't help but notice his cool hairstyle, a long brown bang in front and trimmed hair around the sides. It reminds me of Lance.

"Are you done playing?" he asks.

"We just finished," Kenny says. "The court is yours."

He glances to me.

I like his ocean blue eyes and long, lean legs.

Lowering his racket, he sighs. "Darn, I need a partner for a doubles game."

I swivel back to look at Kenny. He winks and I hand him my cup.

"What's your name?" I ask.

'Chris," he says as I collect my racket and slowly stand to face him. "I've got a strong swing, Chris. You ready to win this?"

"Yeah." His eyes light up.

I wave goodbye to Kenny who shakes his head and laughs as I step back onto the court.

Author's Note

Thank you for reading!

Your feedback is important to me and I want to hear from you. Please feel free to reach out to me at lisavpires@gmail.com or visit my social media pages, Twitter, Facebook, etc. to let me know what you like or what you would like to read about next.

If you enjoyed *Vigil Black*, please consider leaving a review on Amazon or Goodreads.

For more information about L.V. Pires or to sign up for the New Release Mailing List, go to www.lisavpires.com

Welcome back to *The Waiting Mortuary* where being dead doesn't always mean the end.

DEATH WATCH - BOOK 3 of THE WAITING MORTUARY SERIES

It's been a long time since Jack Skilton wrote an article for *The Westport Press*, but when rumors of a sinister presence lurking inside the waiting mortuary begin to spread, he's sent to Kessler's Funeral Home to investigate a possible haunting and what he discovers will definitely make front-page news if only he can live long enough to write about it.

Find out what happens in this horror thriller with supernatural elements written for audiences who enjoy turning pages at breakneck speed. Be warned this story is not for the faint of heart. What begins as a mystery will evolve into total terror.

Don't miss DEATH WATCH, the third book in *The Waiting Mortuary* series by L.V. Pires.

Praise for L.V. Pires:

“This story is like a rollercoaster ride. It builds until total momentum takes you over the edge, screaming and clutching your chest for dear life.” ★★★★★

“Excellent and really gripping.” ★★★★★

“I will definitely recommend this book to lovers of horror and suspense!” ★★★★★

"A very scary ride with an ending to top all others." ★★★★★

"Scariest book I've ever read." ★★★★★

"Huge fan of L.V. Pires! You won't be disappointed." ★★★★★

"Edge-of-my-seat experience! I felt I was living the horror." ★★★★★

"Page-turner with a twist! I was hanging on to every word!" ★★★★★

"One of the greatest suspense-filled books I’ve ever read." ★★★★★

Although in a series, this novel can also **STAND-ALONE**. For fans of Stephen King, Dean Koontz, Richard Laymon, Bentley Little, as well as other horror and mystery authors such as Dan Simmons, Jack Ketchum, Robert McCammon, Brian Keene, Darcy Coates, Amy Cross, Jeff Strand, Ambrose Ibsen, Jeremy Robinson, Nick Cutter, Blake Crouch, Joe Hill, Iain Rob Wright, Jeff Menapace, Matt Shaw, Heather Graham, Jack Kilborn, James Herbert.

Ready for a chilling short story? Try The Portrait
- Available on Kindle/Audible

Karen is an art student attending her first overnight summer camp. She loves being around other artists. Her days are spent drawing, meeting new friends, and fluttering over a super-hot guy who seems to have the same feelings for her. Everything seems to be going well, until she discovers her roommate's unique method for creating art.

A strange infatuation leads to deadly consequences in this spooky tale of horror.

Becca's life is anything but ordinary.

At fifteen, she's already experienced her share of pain. With a mom who drinks too much, a revolving door of father figures, and struggles at school, Becca wonders if she'll ever have a chance at a normal life. The only thing that keeps her sane is her little sister, Chloe; that is until her mother's breakdown leads to her sister's disappearance.

Now, Becca just wants to find her sister, but to do so she'll have to face a family secret head on.

What readers are saying:

"Another fantastic book worth picking up!" - *Amazon Reviewer* ★★★★★

"I loved everything about this book from start to finish it was an overall fantastic read." -*Amazon Reviewer* ★★★★★

"The story is very interesting and it gave me incredible insight into LIFE. I enjoyed this book and would love to read the whole book over and over." -*Amazon Reviewer* ★★★★★

About the Author

With several books in the top 100 U.S. Horror Fiction and Horror Classics categories, award-winning novelist and short story writer, L.V. Pires is the author of terrifying tales that are sure to keep readers up late into the night. Mystery and suspense climax into total terror in this author's upcoming releases.

For more information about this author or to join the mailing list go to www.lisavpires.com

Made in the USA
Columbia, SC
12 October 2020

22695007R00133